Forever Yours, Casey

Cassidy K. O'Connor

Cover Art by Ash Arceneaux

Copyright © 2016 Cassidy K. O'Connor

Dedication

There is nothing more beautiful than the love between a mother and her child.

I am lucky to have three amazing children. They say I can be a 'Mama bear' sometimes and that's okay. That means they know I will always fight for them in any way they need.

Chapter One

Brittany

I can taste the bile rising in my throat as soon as I hear the knock on my door. I've been expecting them but I'm still shaking as I reach for the doorknob. Standing in the doorway are two police officers. I recognize them from the diner and I can tell they aren't happy about doing this either.

"Morning, ma'am. We have a warrant for your arrest."

My shoulders sag in resignation, of course they do. Kacee hears the commotion and runs out of her room yelling.

"No, this isn't fair! He's the creep, why are you arresting her?"

Tears pouring down her face, I squeeze her against me and hold her while she cries. "I'm so sorry, Mommy. This is all my fault."

"Shhh, I'm going to call Grandma and have her come over. Stay here with your brother and get him ready for school. Tell him I had to leave early for work and make sure he gets there. I don't want him at the police station." I grab her face and make her look at me. "Stop crying, baby, we'll get this all sorted out and I'll be home soon."

I swallow the guilt knowing I just lied to my daughter. I know they aren't going to release me anytime soon. I don't have any money or power and they do.

"I'm sorry, ma'am, but we have to handcuff you. You might want to get that call taken care of."

I nod my head and walk with Kacee plastered against my side to the phone. Mom picks up on the first ring sounding worried. People don't usually call before mid-morning unless it's an emergency. I guess this counts as one.

"Hey, Mama, I need you to come over and stay with the kids for a bit. Kacee can explain when you get here."

"I don't understand, what's going on?"

I hear the panic in her voice, but I try to block it out and get off the phone quickly.

"I don't have time to explain, please come over."

"Okay, I'll be there soon."

I hang up, relieved she didn't make me tell her more.

"Okay, baby girl, after you get your brother to school, I need you to tell Grandma what I did then have her find me a lawyer." Her eyes fill with fear; I can imagine how scared she is to retell her story again. "Don't tell her anything but what I did and I'll handle the rest. Ask Mrs. Jennings across the hall to keep Austin when he gets home from school."

I wait for her nod before I step away and hold out my wrists to the police. Their remorseful faces help make this a little easier.

Thank god it's still early and most of the neighbors aren't out yet. I walk quietly to the police car and sit back for the short drive to the station. Looking around, I can't help but be curious about the equipment up front. I wish there wasn't a cage separating me like an animal to be feared. I guess in a way I am; you mess with one of my kids, I am going to come after you.

I'm relieved the police station is mostly empty when we arrive. They process my booking and place me in holding. I haven't said a word other than I am waiting for my lawyer. Two hours I sit on the bench staring at the wall; I'm too scared to think about what is going to happen to the kids if I don't get out. Instead, I sing songs in my head, but by the third round of Maroon 5's "She Will Be Loved" I am ready to climb the walls in frustration. Finally, I hear my mother down the hall yelling at anyone she sees, demanding to see me immediately. One of the cops from this morning comes in with a smirk on his face.

"I'm going to move you to a room so your mother and lawyer can meet with you."

I sag in relief hearing she found a lawyer. I follow meekly down the hall to a small room with a table in the middle and chairs on both sides. I'm surprised there isn't a mirror in here; I've watched so many cop shows I thought that was standard.

Mom is already inside and launches herself at me.

"Brittany, what is going on? They said they are charging you with assault. You've never hurt anyone in your life, this has to be a mistake."

As she speaks, her voice rises higher and higher. I can hear the panic and feel guilt for putting her through another crisis. Why can't I be a good daughter? I shake off my maudlin feelings and turn to the older gentleman standing by the table.

"I sure hope you are my lawyer."

I'm a little concerned at his appearance; he's well past his prime, severely overweight and wearing rumpled clothes. I glance at Mama and she gives me an apologetic shrug. I turn back as he holds his hand out to me. I shake it firmly, ignoring the slimy feeling of his palm.

"My name is Carter Jepsen. Let's talk about what happened and go from there."

In other words, let's find out if your case is worth my time. I sit down and take a deep breath, waiting while they get situated in their chairs. He nods and I start my story.

"I was working at the diner last night when my cell phone started buzzing in my pocket. I was running food and ignored it. When I checked a few minutes later, there were four missed calls, three texts and a voicemail from Kacee. I read the texts first. She said Dirk Montgomery had shown up at 'The Haunt' and was really drunk." I see my mom's eyes widen and Mr. Jepsen's pen pause when I get to Dirk's name. He is obviously considering right then if he should walk away. "Kacee had tried to leave and Dirk wouldn't let her. She had escaped to the bathroom and wanted me to come get her. The voicemail was a sobbing Kacee saying Dirk had attacked her but she had gotten away and was hiding around the corner."

"Why didn't you call the police at that point?"

I give him my best motherly "are you kidding me" look with a quirked eyebrow and tilted head. He clears his throat and has the sense to look sheepish. Everyone in the surrounding area knows the Montgomery's are the most powerful family around. They can pretty much say and do whatever they want with no repercussion. I shake my head and continue on.

"I ran out of there and found her huddling between some cars in the back parking lot. Her shirt was ripped open. I had every intention of taking her home and forgetting about it but when I saw her, I snapped. I put her in the car, locked the doors and stormed in after him." Mama's head is hanging down at this point with tears rolling down her face. I know she is crying for Kacee; I hope none of those tears are because I've shamed her again. "I found him at the bar making out with another girl. I grabbed his shoulder, spun him around and punched as hard as I could. His head snapped back, but he recovered really fast and looked like he was going to hit me so I grabbed a bottle, smashed it against the bar and held it to his throat. I was in a blind rage by that point. I know I screamed some things, but then the bouncers picked me up and tossed me out. I took Kacee home, cleaned her up and put her to bed."

My mother's shoulders are shaking wildly up and down.

"I'm sorry, Mama. I saw her and I couldn't control myself. I know I screwed up again."

Finally, she looks up and I'm shocked into silence. Her tears have turned to laughter she barely contains.

"What I would have given to see you holding a bottle up to that idiot's throat."

"You aren't mad at me?"

"Quite the opposite, I couldn't be prouder. You stood up for your own and there is nothing wrong with that."

The soothing balm of relief flows through my whole body. I didn't realize how worried I was about her reaction till now.

"I know I didn't handle that well..."

Before I can finish my sentence, I yell out in pain. Mama, being proud, had laid her hands over mine and squeezed.

"Ms. Celdonio, have you had your hand looked at since the incident?"

"No, I didn't want to leave Kacee last night. I've been taking pain medicine and babying it the best I could."

"I'm going to have them take you over to the hospital for x-rays, then we'll talk again when you are back."

I take it as a good sign he's still here. He grunts as he stands and waddles over to the door. His knock is immediately answered by the same cop who brought me to the room.

"Hey, Mike, Ms. Celdonio hurt her hand during the incident. Can you run her over to the hospital and get it taken care of?"

"Sure thing, Mr. Jepsen, let me call it in." He turns my way, "I'll be right back to get you."

He smiles as he closes the door. Considering I'm a criminal, I am grateful for the wonderful treatment I'm being given. I know everyone hates the Montgomery family, especially the cops who can't touch them.

"Well, one thing you can be happy about, Dirk turned eighteen last month. At least you didn't assault a minor."

I hadn't even thought of that; this could be so much worse.

"Kacee's out front and she's worried sick. We're going to follow you over to the hospital and she can sit with you while you get taken care of."

The door opens again to my now familiar escort. He shrugs as he holds out the cuffs; I'm grateful that he is being gentle. Mama follows out the hall and squeezes my shoulder as she heads back out front. I'm led out a side door to the waiting police car.

"You should have told us this morning you needed medical attention. We could have taken you to the hospital first."

"I think the adrenaline was still so high, I didn't realize how bad it was till she squeezed it."

He leaned in and buckled me up, whispering in my ear, "Your daughter should be proud of what you did."

I nod and smile sheepishly.

The drive to the hospital is silent. My heartbeat speeds up when I see Kacee standing outside with a nurse and a wheelchair. She looks miserable; I want a do over so badly. I climb in the chair and thank the nurse when she lays a blanket over my handcuffed wrists. As we go inside, I look back and see my escort giving us a lot of space. I guess they really can appreciate what I did.

"I heard you were quite the hero last night. How about we get some x-rays and see if we can't fix you up."

Chapter Two

Casey

I stare at the same spot on the ceiling every morning. I watch as it grows brighter with the sunrise, listening to Monica's soft snores beside me. As the room fully illuminates with the morning rays, my alarm beeps quietly. Mechanically, my arm knows exactly where to move to shut it off, my eyes never leaving that boring spot.

I'm the asshole with the perfect job, perfect condo, perfect fiancée, and absolutely no passion for any of them. I sigh and sit up, I'm just being melancholy. Today is the day I write my annual letter to Brittany. People don't know why this day is important to me, they assume someone close to me died, and I don't blame them, in a way it's true. Fifteen years ago, she disappeared; I've never heard a word from her so how do I know she's alive?

Eight years ago, my therapist convinced me to stop looking for her. I did, but I never stopped writing to the only other person in her life I knew, her grandmother. My letters have never been returned so I assume they are making it there. I used to think about flying out there, pictured walking up the sidewalk and finding Brittany sitting on the porch, drinking a sweet tea and holding out her hand like she's been waiting for me to come find her. I try to block those thoughts now.

My therapist says my obsession is unhealthy. He doesn't know about the letters. For all he knows I'm completely over her. Is it a bad sign when you are lying to your therapist?

My thoughts are interrupted by the hand gliding up my back.

"Good morning, love. I'm going to go make you breakfast while you shower."

"Thanks, babe."

I don't even turn and look at her. How can I when I'm sitting here thinking about another woman?

On auto pilot, I get ready for work and kiss Monica's cheek as I sit at the counter to eat. Very little makes it down, the nerves in my stomach are too amped up. Even though I look miserable, I'm not. I love letter day. I lock myself in my office, pull out a piece of heavy paper and my nicest ball point pen, then pour my heart out to Brittany. I recap everything that has happened since I wrote to her last year. I tell her about new restaurants I've tried, places I've travelled. I ask what she's been up to, and how her mom is, then I pack it up and ship it off, never knowing if it gets there. While Monica is in the shower, I yell out my goodbye and head into the office.

This may all sound creepy but I promise it's not. Everyone has convinced me that she must be dead and I can't bear that thought. I'd rather pretend we're long lost pen pals, albeit a very one-sided relationship.

Walking down the hall, I nod at my secretary and head straight for my office. I'm taken aback when I don't hear the click of my door behind me. I turn and find my secretary following me in. She knows what day it is, my calendar is blocked. What is she doing?

"Do you need something, Mrs. Sampson?"

"I'm sorry, sir, I have a bunch of messages for you from a woman desperate to talk to you."

"Give her to someone else, I'm busy today."

"I tried telling her that, but she said you would want to talk to her. She said her name is Maria Celdonio."

My throat instantly goes dry. Fifteen years to the day and Brittany's mom is calling me. They are alive, I always knew it. As the excitement inside me is building, I remember she said the woman was desperate sounding and it's her mom calling, not her. Dread fills my entire body and I collapse into my chair. Maybe she really is gone.

"Sir, are you all right? Can I get you something? Do you want me to have Mr. Marshall call her back?"

I stand and snatch the papers out of her hand.

"No, I need to call her. Can you make sure I'm not disturbed?"

She nods and slips quietly out the door.

I stare at the phone number; after all this time I have a way of contacting them. Once the Internet became available, I spent months looking for them but never found a trace. Right after college this firm hired me, they have a team of private investigators at their disposal. I considered using them many times, but my therapist was right. I was obsessing and I needed to move on. If she wanted to be found, she wouldn't be hiding so well.

I reach a trembling hand to the phone and dial slowly, as if I'm scared it's all a joke and she won't pick up the phone. My stomach clenches when a soft voice picks up on the first ring.

"Hi, my name is Casey Sanders. I'm trying to reach..."

"Casey, thank god you called me back. I know you have a lot of questions," now that she is talking, I recognize Mrs. Celdonio's voice. "I know we took off on you all those years ago and I'm sorry for that, but Brittany needs you. She's in a lot of trouble and I don't think I can help her this time."

I jump out of my chair involuntarily, my body ready for action. Every fiber of my being is pulsing now that I know she is alive.

"What happened, where is she?"

"She's in jail, they won't let me bond her out and her court hearing is tomorrow." Her voice cracks as she continues on, "I don't think they are going to let her out and I don't know what to do."

"Tell me where you are and I can be there today."

Nerves tingle through my body. This torturous mystery will finally be over.

"We're in Salt Lake City, Utah."

A grim look crosses my face. She's in the same city I've been sending those letters to. Has she been getting them all this time? I'll add that to my list of questions when I see her. "Give me her lawyer's name and I'll get things started while I'm on the plane."

"Well, Carter Jepsen saw her this morning but he hasn't agreed to take her case yet. Honestly, I don't think I'm going to find anyone in the area to help us."

"Why the hell not?" What could she possibly have done to make her case untouchable?

"She pissed off the Montgomery family and they run things around here. Nobody wants to get on their bad side."

I can't help but chuckle, "Of course that wouldn't stop Britt from standing up to them."

"I promise you she did it for the right reasons. If you can forgive us for taking off on you all those years ago, we would be grateful for your help."

"It's not even a question, I'll be there by tonight. As soon as I have my flight information, I will text it to you. Is this your cell phone number?"

"Yes, let me know when you get in and I'll meet you at the jail."

"Sounds good, and Maria, thank you for calling."

I slam the phone down and run out the door.

"Leslie, I have a family emergency and need to take off for a few days. I am going home to pack. I need you to book me the next flight out to Salt Lake City and get me a car and a hotel near the courthouse. Check what the state law is to let me practice out there. Also, look up Carter Jepsen, he's a lawyer out there. Text me his address and phone number."

I wait long enough to see she has written all my instructions down before I bolt out the door. On the drive home, I call Monica. I vaguely tell her an old family friend from high school is in trouble and I need to leave. Like the perfect fiancée she is, she tells me she loves me and says she will miss me.

Forty-five minutes later, I have an email with a detailed travel itinerary, and Mr. Jepsen's number. Best of all, Utah practices Pro Hac Vice so all I need besides some paperwork is a lawyer to sponsor me. Thank god for Leslie and her exceptional organizational skills. I grab my bags and head for the door. Waiting outside is a car service; I really need to give Leslie a raise. The ride gives me time to leave a message for Mr. Jepsen asking him to meet me at the jail tonight. Emotions flood my brain. Leaning against the headrest, I let my mind drift back to the last time I saw her.

Chapter Three

Brittany

July 1990

"Have you told your parents about our plan yet?"

My stomach clenches when I feel him tense against me. That's not a good sign.

"I'm sorry, Britt, I will soon. Turning down Harvard so I can go to State with you is going to be hard for them to accept. Add to that us moving in together and they will explode."

I close my eyes so he can't see the pain I'm trying to hide. I feel his hand grab my chin and turn my face toward him.

"You are perfect, don't take it personally. They are elitists and in a few months, I will be free of their control. My scholarship means I don't need any of their money. We'll both get jobs and manage just fine."

Shaking my head, I pull away. "This is crazy. Your parents are right, you should be at Harvard."

His arms envelop me; I can't resist leaning back against his warm chest.

"What's really going on? You have been all over the place lately."

"I'm sorry, I'm scared you are going to wake up six months after we're living together and regret it." I can't help the tingle running down my body when he kisses my neck.

"You are the only good thing in my life; I wish we were already living together. Senior year starts in a few weeks, let me hold off telling them as long as possible. We'll have a lot more fun if I'm not grounded the entire time."

Before I can respond, the alarm next to my bed blares, reminding us we have to get dressed before my mom comes home.

We scramble to get ready and sit down in front of the TV in the living room when I hear her keys jingle at the door. I give him one more quick kiss as the door opens revealing my exhausted mother.

"Hey, Mom, how was work?"

She collapses into the recliner, her head immediately falling backward.

"It must be a full moon since every crazy in the city was in the café tonight. Joe had to kick a guy out who kept grabbing my butt." She peeks one eye at us, "If he was a prince I might have let him, but this guy was a total frog."

"I wish you would quit that place, it's so gross."

Casey jumps up and heads for the kitchen, coming back with the plate of dinner we had saved for her. I love that he can see exactly what my mom needs.

"Here you go, ma'am."

"Casey Sanders, I have known you for a year now. We are way past the ma'am stage, aren't we? And please lord tell me this is your cooking and not hers."

I feign shock and hurt that quickly turns to laughter. It's no secret I can't even boil water well.

"This is my concoction but she supervised."

She takes a bite and moans. "Oh my god, Casey, I am sure going to miss your food when you leave for Harvard."

She's so involved in her food she doesn't even notice the look he gives me. His eyes bulge and I can read the accusation in them. An hour ago I was yelling at him for keeping it a secret and now he knows I have been, too. Honestly, I haven't told her yet for the same reasons. Everyone knows he is the smartest guy in our town and he deserves to get out of here. She wants him to go and make something of himself. I hate myself for keeping him here. I've tried convincing him we can date long distance but he won't hear it. I could go to a community college near Harvard but the out-of-state tuition would be ridiculous and I can't leave my mom here alone.

I get up to grab a drink for her and he follows me into the kitchen. Out of the corner of my eye, I see him leaning against the counter with his arms crossed. Stalling long enough, I grab a Coke and turn to give him my most angelic look possible. He has one eyebrow up, just staring at me.

"What? I'm going to tell her eventually. I don't want to listen to her bitch at me for keeping you here."

He's still not melting, so I kiss him softly all around his face till I feel him relax and take a deep breath.

"You're lucky you're so cute."

I smile and spin on my heel, as I get to the door he smacks my butt playfully. The snores coming from the couch stop us both. I hate seeing her so rundown all the time.

"I wish she would let me get a job so she can quit one of hers."

"She wants you focusing on school, not worrying about money." He turns me around and wipes a tear from the corner of my eye. "You are going to get that scholarship and she won't have to worry about saving up anymore. Keep volunteering and doing everything they want. It will be over soon and she can finally relax."

I nod and let him hug me till I get my tears under control.

"Do you need help getting her in bed before I go?"

"No, I'm okay. I'll see you on Saturday?"

"Of course, nothing could keep me from you."

Chapter Four

Casey

"Britt, Mrs. Celdonio, anyone home?"

I bang on the door again. Where are they? We were supposed to hang out on Saturday but I haven't heard from her in two days.

Frustrated, I head to the free clinic where Britt's been volunteering. The waiting room is packed with screaming babies and tired looking parents. I head to the counter where I usually see Britt sitting and wait to be acknowledged. The woman is busy typing, talking on the phone and trying to move files from pile to pile. She finally hangs up and gives me a weary look.

"Can I help you, son?"

"Hi, I'm Brittany Celdonio's boyfriend. I haven't been able to reach her in a few days. I was hoping I could talk to her for a minute?"

"You and me both, sweetie. She didn't show up this morning," the phone rings, grabbing her attention. "I gotta go but when you find her, can you remind her she needs to call in if she's sick?"

"I'll let her know, thanks."

That little nagging feeling I've been ignoring in the pit of my stomach grows ten times bigger. Desperate to find her, I head for her mom's night job at the café.

I suppress the shiver going down my back when I arrive. This place is a dump; I don't blame Britt for wanting her mom out of here. We've been here a few times to keep an eye on her so Joe knows me well enough. I find him sitting behind the cash register reading a magazine.

"I'm surprised to see you here. I figured with the girls being gone you wouldn't step back into this place."

That lump in my stomach is now suffocating me.

"What do you mean they're gone?"

He smiles big, showing off the gaps between his teeth.

"Oh, they didn't tell you they were leaving?"

Pain radiates up my arm as I slam my fist on the counter.

"What do you mean they're gone?"

"Okay, okay, relax, kid. Maria came in Saturday morning and asked for her pay, said she was sorry to leave me high and dry but she needed to take care of her family. I'm real sorry to see her go, she was a hard worker. Hey, man, you okay? You need some water?"

I shake my head and stumble out of the restaurant and back to my car. I don't even remember driving back to their apartment. I stare at the door to their building, willing one of them to walk out. After a few hours, I give up and go home.

I go back every day, knock and wait. I sit against their door and wait. Finally, on Saturday, I see the superintendent coming up the stairs.

"Excuse me, I was wondering if you could tell me where the Celdonio's from 3b went?"

"Yeah, you must be the boyfriend. I heard you've been hanging around here. Listen, kid, I'm sorry to tell you this but they are gone. They took off over the weekend, gave up their security and everything. Something got them spooked to leave that quick."

"Did they tell you where they were going?"

"I didn't ask." He shrugs and I fight to stay calm.

"Do you think you could let me in for a minute? I want to see if Britt left anything for me."

I think he could see the desperation on my face. He squeezed my shoulder and walked over to their door. I watched him swing it open, then he stood back to let me in but I froze. I didn't know what I was going to find and that scared me more than anything.

"They aren't in there, go ahead."

I walk in like I have a hundred times before, but this time there is barren furniture. The photo frames with our prom pictures are gone, the blanket her grandmother had crocheted for her isn't hanging over the back of the couch.

My feet shuffle across the wood floor toward her room. My eyes fill with tears seeing the barren room. Her furniture is there but like the rest of the house, everything personal is gone. My heart starts racing and bile rises in my throat as I run to the desk and tear open the drawers. Empty, everything is empty. Falling on to the bed, I hear a noise when my head hits the heart pillow I had given her. Why would she leave that? Eagerly I reach under and find a partial piece of paper, the edges torn raggedly, and I want to throw up when I read her beautiful cursive handwriting.

> *I'm sorry I didn't say goodbye. It's better for you this way. I wish all the best for you. I know you will do awesome at Harvard. All my love, B*

Tear drops land on the paper before I realize they are coming from me. I don't understand, none of this makes sense. We had a plan, what changed?

Chapter Five

Brittany

Current Day 2005

My new blue cast is large and bulky. It's bad enough I am in jail but to now be down one hand will be almost intolerable. I tried to get a plain white one but Kacee wouldn't hear of it. She made them give me my favorite color. I know she feels horrible about my broken fingers. If only she understood I would sacrifice my whole arm before letting something happen to her.

"You're all set, ma'am. I'm going to get your discharge paperwork and you'll be on your way."

I nod, still numb to the idea of going back to my cell. I paste on my best smile and turn to Kacee.

"At dinner tonight, I'm going to have Mama tell Austin what is happening. I know it's going to upset him but I don't believe in lying either. I need you to be positive and help him through this. I see the judge tomorrow morning, I'm sure I'll be home before school gets out."

It's not technically lying if I choose to believe it too, right?

Officer Freeman comes back with the nurse. He cuffs my good hand to the chair and lays the blanket over it. I smile as he stands back and waits for us to get ahead before he leaves the room. I kiss Kacee goodbye as Mama comes walking down the hall. The smile on her face is so hopeful my heart squeezes. Maybe this nightmare is over?

"I found another lawyer to help out Mr. Jepsen. We're going to meet tonight at six o'clock."

"Oh, well that's good, I guess."

"Don't look so crestfallen, everything is going to be all right."

I nod so I don't look ungrateful. So much for thinking she performed a miracle and got me out.

"I'll get the kids situated for dinner then I'll be back with some clothes for tomorrow."

"Thank you for everything. I really am sorry to put you through this."

She waves off my apology and takes Kacee out the front entrance of the hall.

On the short ride back to the station, I contemplate my new lawyer. If she found someone to be excited about, she must have gone outside the city. I know everyone is scared of the Montgomery's, I should be grateful I got anyone to even listen to me.

As I'm placed back in my cell, an officer comes by with a tray of food. My stomach growls at the sandwich and potato chips on a paper plate and a paperback of one of those steamy romance books. I smile at the cop who winks and heads out. I am lucky to have them on my side if no one else.

Wearily, I drop down onto my cot and eat quickly. With little else to do till my meeting tonight, I lie down and get lost reading *Lady Marshman and the Swashbuckling Pirate Deveroux*. It sounds cheesy and exciting all at once, a perfect story to kill time with.

Eight chapters in, the pirate is about to take Lady Marshman for his own when I hear keys rattle and my door open. It's the same officer who lent me the book.

"Thank you for letting me read this. I'd probably be losing my mind in here without it."

"Not a problem, my wife always says a good book can make any problem seem insignificant. I figured you could use the distraction and it looks like it worked, your lawyers are here to meet with you."

I stand and smooth my hair as I follow him down the hall to the same room from this morning. The door is open; my mother is standing in the doorway looking anxious.

"I'm sorry to surprise you like this but it's for the best."

My look of confusion turns to shock as I look inside and see the most beautiful sight in the world. My love is standing next to the table, holding his breath and staring at me. I didn't think I'd ever see him again and now he's here. My knees buckle and I lean against my mom, my questioning eyes turning to her.

"I kept tabs on him, he's a big shot lawyer now. If anyone can get you out of this, it's him. I'm sorry I didn't say something earlier but I wasn't sure you would want his help."

Every day for the last fifteen years he has been my last thought before going to sleep. There has always been a part of me that has wanted to run back to him. Of course she's talking about the other part of me, the part that knows he will hate me when he finds out why we left. This thought turns my insides cold; a moment ago I was going to crush him in a hug and likely blubber all over his expensive looking suit, but now I don't know how to act.

"Britt?"

I hear the hesitation in his voice; he looks as confused as I feel. He takes a step toward me. I circle quickly so I can sit across the table. If I touch him, I might shatter, and what kind of self-respecting woman would I look like then?

Mr. Jepsen recognizes the awkwardness of the situation and clears his throat.

"How about we have a seat and get everyone caught up?"

I stare at the table, not able to make eye contact with him yet. I watch both lawyers uncap their pens. Casey clears his throat and out of the corner of my eye I can see he's confused by my behavior.

"On the plane ride up here I got a basic report. It says you assaulted a young man in a place called 'The Haunt.' The report says nothing as to what prompted the incident. What caused the altercation?"

I look over at Mama, who nods her head sadly. She knows what I'm about to tell him is going to crush him. I straighten my spine and look him square in the eye.

"I had been at work when I got some messages from my daughter saying she had been attacked by that scum bag. I went over to get her and my rage took over. I punched him and threatened him if he went near her again."

I can see the wheels spinning in his head.

"You have a daughter...how old is she?"

I swallowed the bile rising up my throat.

"Her name is Kacee and she is fifteen."

I look down and see his knuckles have turned white around the pen. Mr. Jepsen continues on for me, bless him and his ignorance of the undercurrents swarming around us.

"Ms. Celdonio did not file a report about her daughter's attack. I'm afraid we have a pretty tough case against us."

I glance over, surprise written on my face. The way he had acted this morning, I figured there was no way he was going to take my case. He picks up on my questioning look.

"I'm retiring in a couple of months and moving to Florida, I figure they can't do much to me if I'm not around anymore. Plus, from what I hear, Mr. Sanders here is a shoo-in for District Attorney back in South Carolina. If anyone has a shot at beating them, it's him."

I can't help the huge smile on my face, momentarily I forget the bomb I just dropped on him.

"You did it? You went to Harvard?"

He hasn't moved a muscle.

"Mr. Jepsen, how about you and I step outside for a few minutes. I think they have some talking to do." Mama squeezes my shoulder and leads the way out. The tiny room actually feels smaller now that we're alone.

My eyes slowly drag from the door back to his face. His eyes boring into mine cause a shiver down my spine. "I'm sorry."

He huffs and shakes his head. "Should I assume her birthday is six to eight months from now?"

"Yes, she is your daughter and her birthday is in seven months."

"Jesus, Britt, how could you do this?"

He jumps out of his chair, pacing the room.

"It was better this way."

"Is that what you tell yourself so you can sleep better at night? I thought you were dead and all this time you were here raising our child? I never forgot you, I never could accept that you were gone, and now I find out you had moved on without me?"

"Look at you now, Casey, you have everything you deserve. If I had stayed, you wouldn't have gone to college and made something for yourself. It was for the best..."

"Stop saying that! That is the lie you tell yourself to feel less guilty."

The anguish on his face is devastating and his shoulders are rising rapidly with fast breaths. I did this to him, I hurt him all over again. "You're right, we had no right to keep her from you."

Standing up, I want to go to him. I want to hug him and take his pain away. I take one step forward and he jerks back like I'm a snake going to bite him.

"Just let me absorb all this, I need time to think."

I swallow hard and nod. He opens the door and waves everyone else back in. Mama gives me a sympathetic look before sitting down.

Casey sits down, gracefully picks up his pen like I didn't just alter his entire life, and continues on.

"I presume you've never had any other run ins with the law?"

I quirk my eyebrow at his surly tone. "No, I've never been in trouble before. I'm on the PTA at school, the worst I've done is return a library book a few days late."

"That all works in our favor." He turns to Mr. Jepsen, "Do you have a list of witnesses to the event? I'd like to know what we're up against."

"I'll email you everything I have and tell the boys to give you access to everything else."

"All right then, I have my homework to do tonight." His eyes lock on me again and I can't help the shiver running down my spine, "You get a good night's sleep and in the morning, prepare yourself to look as small and defenseless as possible for the judge."

I nod and watch sadly as he packs his briefcase and walks out without another look toward me.

"I agree with Mr. Sanders, rest up tonight and we'll get you out of here tomorrow."

"Thank you for agreeing to stay on and help me."

He gives me a fatherly smile and walks out. Mama engulfs me in a hug; even at my age it is amazing how much that helps.

"I'm sure that was hard but it needed to be done. I had to call him, I didn't think we stood a chance otherwise."

I could tell she thought I was mad; she's waiting for me to break down.

"I'm glad you called him and you are right, we do need him."

"I'll be back in the morning, try not to dwell too much on the past tonight."

She knows me too well. How can I not think about the beautiful boy that turned into the gorgeous man I saw tonight? Every emotion I've had bottled up for the last fifteen years is pulsing through my body and I'm stuck alone in a cell for the next fourteen hours.

Returning to my cell, I find my dinner tray waiting next to the pirate book I was enthralled with earlier. Thank god eating is an automatic response or I don't know how the food would have gotten into my mouth. With the first bite of the rubbery meatloaf, my mind travels back to the day everything changed all those years ago.

Chapter Six

Brittany

July 1990

"Honey, have you seen my black cardigan…Jesus, Brittany, what's wrong with your stomach?"

I freeze while pulling my shirt over my head. I take it back off and stare at my stomach, expecting to see a cut or bruise.

"What's on me, what's wrong?"

Her hand is shaking as she reaches out and pushes on my belly in a few places.

"When's the last time you had your period?"

"I don't know, a few weeks ago?"

"When, Brittany? Think about it, have you gotten it at all this summer?"

Thinking back to school ending in May, I remember having it on the last day but not since then. My eyes bulge and my face feels like it's on fire. Panicked, I look at her.

"Shit, Brittany! I'll be back in a few minutes."

She storms out of my room and I collapse on my bed when I hear the door to our apartment slam shut. Staring at my belly, I notice it has gotten a little bigger. I poke it, it's firm. Last time I checked, I didn't have any muscles there. This can't be happening.

Five minutes later, two of my fingernails are chewed down to nubs. I hear the door to the apartment and run out to the living room. A paper bag is thrown at me without a word. Slinking off to the bathroom, I pull the box out and stare at it. I'm sure these things are easy enough to figure out but I read the directions anyways. I guess I'm really putting off the inevitable.

With a heavy sigh and a shaky hand, I pee on the stick and set it on the wrapper. I chew another fingernail while staring intently at that stupid little display box, willing it to show a negative sign. The box said wait three to five minutes, but not even two minutes in and the cursed plus sign appears. Numbly, I grab the stick and open the door. She's standing there staring intently.

"Mommy..." I burst into tears as her arms envelop me.

"It's okay, baby, I'll take care of everything."

"Casey is going to freak, and his parents, they are going to hate me even more."

She leans back and holds my face between her hands.

"Casey can't know, none of them can. We're going to pack up and leave for Grandma's."

I can't hide the horror on my face.

"What are you talking about? I need to tell him; I can't just take off."

"That boy has a real shot of making something for himself. Your life is already ruined, don't take him down, too."

I jerk out of her arms. "Is that what happened to you? Did I ruin your life?"

"No, sweetie, you are the greatest gift in my life. This baby will be just as special. I just meant your plans are changing now and we both know Casey won't go to Harvard if you are here with his baby. You need to let him go be somebody, let him make something of himself."

She's right, she isn't saying anything I haven't been thinking for weeks now already. "You're right, it's better if we leave."

"I'm going to run over to the market and grab some boxes. We can only take what we can fit in the car so start cleaning out your room."

Still shocked this is really happening, I nod and head off to my room. I grab all the pictures of Casey and wrap them in shirts. I'm only going to get through this if I stop thinking about him.

When the last picture is put away and the tears start falling, I give in and let the wracking sobs come. I open my eyes when I feel the bed sink a little. For a fleeting second I hope its Casey and he'll stop this from happening. Instead, it's my mother's sad eyes. She lies next to me and lets me finish crying.

Once the hiccups replace the sobs, she sits back up.

"It will get easier, Brittany, but for now you take it one minute, one hour, one day at a time. We'll get through this together. Now, let's get packing, I want to be on the road by seven a.m."

******

We work till three in the morning. Sixteen years in that apartment, we accumulated a lot of crap. I only break down crying once. Mama never cried in front of me but I heard her sobbing when she called Grandma and told her.

One last look around the apartment before heading out leaves my heart breaking. It's an empty shell of our home. Even the furniture looks sad, betrayed that we're leaving it behind.

"Come on, baby, I need to stop by the café before we go."

With a final slam of the door, we leave for the last time. Hugging my book to my chest, I climb in the stuffed wagon, put on my sunglasses and try to fall asleep.

The next four days pass slowly. I take turns driving, we sleep at rest areas along the way and I do everything I can to ignore the pain in my chest. I feel horrible leaving without seeing Casey first. I pray he found the note I hid for him. Mama questioned why I left the heart pillow Casey had given me, but she easily accepted my excuse that I didn't want the reminder.

We pull into Grandma's driveway before dinner time. I haven't been here since I was a kid. It's a cute two story house. I remember the first time I visited, I thought it was a mansion.

"You made it!"

The excitement on Grandma's face as she comes barreling out the front door makes me feel a little bad we haven't been here in a while. Her arms swallow me in a breathless hug and I'm surprised by the feeling of safety I feel immediately. Maybe everything is going to be all right after all.

"Come on, let's get you guys settled in then we'll have dinner. We have a lot to talk about."

Chapter Seven

Casey

Present Day (2005)

I have a kid, not a kid but a teenager. When she first walked into that room, it took everything I had not to pounce on her. If Mr. Jepsen hadn't been in the room, I probably would have. I was surprised by the shock on her face; it hurt a little that she didn't know to call me. I guess she never kept tabs on me like her mom apparently did.

My thoughts of betrayal, hurt, love, and lust are disrupted by my phone ringing.

"Hello?"

"I hear you are helping that bitch, Brittany. You may want to get out of town now if you know what's good for you."

"What makes you think I would be scared of a chicken shit who doesn't even have the guts to threaten me in person? I'm staying at the Hilton by the airport if you have the balls to come here."

I hit the end call button and resist the urge to throw it. I have no doubt who that is, and I'm shocked how fast he got my number. I only gave it to Jepsen and the police, which means they have someone on the inside.

I dial up Jepsen, and he picks up on the second ring.

"Hey, Sanders, did you get all the files you needed?"

"Yeah, I got everything before I left the station. Listen, I got a neighborly call from someone suggesting I quit the case. Do we need to worry Brittany isn't safe tonight?"

"Shit, these guys work fast. Most of the force is on our side. They hate this family as much as we do. I don't know who the moles are but trust me when I tell you there are enough on our side to take care of her tonight. Before I left I made sure Steve would keep an eye on her. He used to date my daughter and I trust him completely."

I've been doing this job enough years that I trust my gut, and he sounds legit.

"Thanks for doing that. Are you all set for the morning? If we can't get the case thrown out, I will post bail for her. What about this Judge Peters, where are his loyalties?"

"He's always been a decent guy; he lets some of their dirty work slide by but I don't think he's going to be a hard ass on Ms. Celdonio."

"Let's hope not. I'm going to finish up reading these files then get a few hours' sleep. I'll see you at the station in the morning."

We hang up and I toss the phone on the bed. After a quick shower, I grab the stack of witness accounts and dig in.

It doesn't take me long to realize every story is identical. Apparently every single person interviewed saw the exact same thing, heard the same words and all claim Kacee was never there. They claim Brittany was a mad woman who attacked for no reason at all. Awfully convenient that everyone saw the same thing no matter where they were in the noisy, dark club.

With a frustrated sigh, I shove my notes into my briefcase and try to get some sleep. Apparently I'm taking on a mob tomorrow.

Chapter Eight

Brittany

"Rise and shine, ma'am. Your mother has clothes for you to change into then we'll get you over to your hearing."

I smile at the female guard and follow her down the hall to the same room I've been in the last two days. I smile at the floral 1950s looking dress lying on the table; it will definitely make me look feminine and motherly.

I finish quickly and knock on the door to let them know I'm finished. I follow the guard down another hall and after a few more turns, I realize we've passed from the police station to the courthouse. Nerves suddenly attack, my hands feel sweaty and my stomach rolls.

We turn a corner and I see Mr. Jepsen and Casey waiting outside a door. Casey in his suit with his briefcase makes my stomach roll for a different reason. I've never been interested in suits before but my entire body tingles with desire.

I shake my head; I know it's been a while but now is not the time to think about this.

"Ms. Celdonio, you look lovely. Might I suggest you change focus a little and work to look timid and fragile? Make people think there is no way you could threaten or harm that idiot."

I nod, embarrassed that my emotions must have been obvious on my face. I've never been good at hiding them. It only takes one look into my eyes to know exactly how I feel.

With a deep breath, I compose myself and nod again to let them know I'm ready. The door opens and all heads turn to look at me. I see Dirk and his goons sitting behind the prosecutor. He blows a kiss at me and my fists bunch. A large, warm hand squeezes my shoulder and I glance over at Casey. He mimics a deep breath; I nod sheepishly and scan the rest of the room. Tears well up when I see Mama sitting behind the table I'm heading toward. She nods and smiles, it gives me strength to know she is on my side.

Taking my place, I look up to the judge and swallow the bile rising in my throat. This is really happening.

I listen as the charges are read, resisting the urge to bite my nail.

"How does the defendant plead?"

Casey looks down at me and nods.

"Not guilty, your Honor."

We all turn when Dirk let's out a loud laugh, his goons are chuckling as well.

"Your honor, we have multiple witnesses who will testify that this was an unprovoked attack. We are asking bail be withheld."

I turn to Casey, shocked. I never thought they would keep me here till the trial. Tears roll down my face as Casey reaches under the table and squeezes my hand.

He stands up and clears his throat.

"Your Honor, Ms. Celdonio is a loving, single mother. She works full-time and has never been in any kind of trouble. She does not have a passport and all her family lives here as well. She is not a flight risk and refusing bail is completely uncalled for."

The judge stares intently at Casey, who is radiating control and power. Those tingly feelings are back and stronger than ever.

"All right, I'll set the bond for $500,000 and the condition that you are personally responsible for her till the trial."

He smacks the gavel and calls for the next case. Casey turns a smiling face to me; he seems proud but I can't understand why.

"I can't believe they are keeping me here. I need to get home."

"Everything is fine, you'll be home tonight."

"Maybe you didn't hear him but he set the bail for half a million dollars. You said yourself I'm a single mother, I don't have that kind of money and I don't own anything I can sell."

He grabs my shoulders and forces me to stare at him.

"You don't need to do anything. I'm going to head over to the bondsman now and I'll have you out in a couple of hours."

He turns and heads out of the room without a second glance. My attention is caught by Dirk staring me down. He isn't very happy with the judge's decision either.

"Let's get you back to the jail."

I smile and wave to Mama and follow the guard out the side door again.

"Mr. Jepsen, he doesn't have to pay the whole amount, does he?"

"No, they will ask for ten percent."

"I still can't even pay that much."

"Mr. Sanders has got it; he came prepared for this. Give it a couple of hours and you'll be with your kids."

I stop and grab his hand.

"Thank you for sticking by me. I know the risk you are taking and I want you to know how appreciative I am."

"You're welcome and the way I figure it, why not go out in a blaze of glory?"

While I don't agree with his sentiment, I appreciate it still. I nod and follow the guard back to my cell. She announces I don't need to change since Casey has already started the process to get me out. With nothing else to do, I lay down and finish the pirate book. I need to know if the damsel made an honest man of the rapscallion or did she join him on his boat.

As I get to the last page, my cell opens and the female officer announces it's time to go. I hold my finger up and race to get to the end. With a satisfied huff, I slam the book closed and pop up excitedly.

"You would be the first person to ever ask me to wait to release you."

"I'm a career reader, what can I say? I can't leave the book unfinished. Can you give this back to Officer Freeman and thank him for me? I probably would have gone crazy in here without this."

"I'll let him know."

Casey is waiting at the processing station. I smile timidly and avoid eye contact after that. I follow him out to his car and thank him when he holds the door open for me. It's been a long time since anyone has done that for me.

He slides into the driver's seat and grips the steering wheel hard.

"Thank you..."

"Listen, Brittany..."

We chuckle and he gestures for me to go first.

"Thank you for doing this. I would still be in there if it weren't for you. It will take me a while but I promise I'll pay you back."

"Let's worry about that later. Since I'm personally responsible for you and you pissed off some pretty bad guys, I'm moving you and Kacee to the hotel with me. I've rented a two room suite, you two can stay in one and I'll be in the other."

My face pales.

"Now would probably be a good time to tell you I have a son as well."

"Is he mine, too? Are they twins?"

"Oh no, sorry, he is seven. His dad left right after he was born. He decided fatherhood wasn't for him."

"It's a good thing that room has two queen beds then. Look, I'm not going to pretend I'm okay with all of this. Let's take it one day at a time and see how it goes."

I nod, grateful he isn't going to turn tail and run.

"I sent your mother ahead to get the kids packed and don't worry, I'm not going to reveal who I am to Kacee right away. We can do it later."

My shoulders sag with relief. I hadn't figured out how I was going to break the news to her yet.

Ten silent minutes later, we pull up to my building. Casey jogs around and opens my door; I freeze as I climb out.

"What's wrong?"

"Dirk is in the black car across the street."

His head swings around in time to see Dirk smile and wave before peeling out.

"This kid is going to be a pain in my ass. Jepsen mentioned he's eighteen now, that means he's not in school anymore, right?"

"He graduated last year so there's no reason for him to go there."

"Good, we should probably call both kids' schools and ask them to be aware of the case and the restraining order we're going to file against Dirk for Kacee." He grabs my hand and squeezes, "I promise, Brittany, nothing is going to happen to any of you while I'm here."

I hide my smile; his worry gives me hope that he will forgive me.

He follows me up the stairs. I open the door and get crushed by Austin. With him holding on, I shuffle in and let Casey inside. Mama gives me a hug and yells to Kacee that I'm home. She runs out of her room and stops dead.

"Daddy?"

Chapter Nine

Casey

Time stops...my heart stops...this beautiful girl that has my same black hair and blue eyes slaps her hand over her mouth and looks shocked.

"Kacee Elizabeth, you know who this is?"

With tear-filled eyes, she nods.

"Explain yourself right now."

"How about we all sit down and get comfortable first?" Brittany's pale face turns to me; it takes her a second to process what I said. She nods and I follow her to the living room.

Kacee sits on the edge of the recliner biting her nail. I know exactly where she got that habit from. Briefly I wonder which habits of mine she inherited.

"Mama, did you do this? Did you tell her about him?"

Maria shakes her head emphatically.

"No one told me anything. Last summer when we spent the week at Great-Grandma's, I was playing hide and seek with Austin. I hid in her closet, the lights were out and when I shifted around, I knocked some shoe boxes over. When I turned on the light to clean them up, I found a bunch of letters addressed to you." She stands up and starts pacing in front of us. "I was flipping through them and I saw they were all from the same person, the mail stamps on them showed they had been coming since I was born. I couldn't help it, I opened them and read every one."

Some of my anger toward Brittany dissipates. I feel a little better that she hadn't been reading my letters all these years and ignoring me.

"You've been writing to me all this time?"

"I never forgot you. But I don't understand, why didn't your grandmother give you the letters?"

"I'm afraid that's my fault."

We all turned surprised eyes to Maria.

"Brittany, you were so depressed those first few months, you cried all the time. I knew those letters would make it harder for you to stay away. I did what I thought was best."

Brittany is shaking her head, the confusion written all over her face.

"Kacee, why didn't you tell me about the letters when you found them?"

"I stayed in that closet for hours reading those letters over and over. It didn't take me long to figure out you had taken off on him while pregnant with me and you named me after him. It was surreal watching my dad grow up through these letters. The pain, love and desperation were almost painful to read."

I look down at my shoes. It's embarrassing now to hear someone else talk about the things I wrote in there.

"You never talked about my dad. I could always pick up on the pain it caused you just by me mentioning him, plus at first I felt greedy. I didn't want to share him with anyone else."

Her voices cracks on the last word and Brittany stands up and hugs her. Part of me wants to do the same but I don't know if any of us are ready for that. Once their tears have slowed down, Kacee starts again.

"Once we got home, I looked him up on the internet and found out everything I could about him. I found an engagement announcement and articles about him running for District Attorney. I realized he had a whole life of his own and I had no right to get in the way."

At that statement, I stood. "You would never be in the way. Now that I know about you, I promise I will always be a part of your life."

She runs into my arms and at first I stand there stunned, then finally my brain kicks in and I wrap my arms around her.

"Are you my daddy, too?"

Austin is sitting on the floor next to the couch, his little face staring up at me intently. I'm not sure what to say, but luckily Brittany steps in.

"No, baby, he's not."

His sad face looks to the floor.

I move Kacee back so I can kneel next to him and get his attention.

"The way I see it, you have been here helping take care of my daughter so that makes you very important to me. It would make me very happy if you would let me be your friend."

"Are you going to take them away from me?"

My heart breaks for this confused little boy. I know exactly how it feels to be abandoned and I don't want him ever thinking he will be.

"Actually, I rented a really big suite at a hotel and I thought we could all go stay there for a while and get to know each other." Austin still looks unsure whether he can trust me. "We can order room service whenever we want and they have a big pool with a slide."

His face lights up with excitement, I think he's past his fear.

"Come on, Austin, let's go finish packing."

I smile at Maria as she grabs his hand and leads him to his room.

"Thank you for doing that, I've tried to get his dad to see him but he's not interested."

"His loss is my gain."

She turns back to Kacee and clears her throat.

"Do you have the letters here?"

"No, I didn't want Great-Grandma to find them gone so I took pictures of them and put them back."

Relief washes over me instantly. I would be mortified to have her whip them out so Brittany could start reading them. I bared my soul in those letters and I am too emotionally raw right now to go through that.

"Kacee, can you finish packing so we can leave soon?"

She nods shyly and leaves; being alone with Brittany this time is even more awkward. My mind is at war with my heart. Part of me wants to be angry and hate her for everything she has denied me all this time. The other part of me wants to hold her and kiss her like I have been dreaming of for the last fifteen years. I'm not an idiot, I know I need to let go of the anger because I've already missed enough, but I'm not sure I can yet.

"I can't believe you've been writing to me all these years and they never told me. I get why they didn't in the beginning but now, after all this time?"

"I don't think either of us can be mad at them, they did what they thought was best for us. It was shitty and wrong but I get it."

She steps toward me and rests her tiny, pale hand on my forearm. How badly I want to crush her against me. I can read the longing in her eyes, and I'm sure she can read the pain mixed with desire in mine.

"Everyone's packed and ready to go."

The spell is broken as Maria stands in the doorway with the kids. Austin is carrying his teddy bear, smiling from ear to ear. He looks excited about our adventure. Kacee stands there casting hopeful glances between her mother and me.

I grab Kacee's duffle bag from her and reach for Brittany's bag sitting by the couch. It's a quiet walk to the car. We say goodbye to Maria with the promise that we will check in often.

After the bags are packed, I slam the trunk shut and pause at the sight in front of me...my family sitting in the car waiting for me. I have a whole other life back home with an awesome fiancée and the job I've been working toward my whole life, but right in front of me is the love of my life, my daughter and a boy I could easily love as if he were my own. Shaking my head, I clear my thoughts. I don't have time to figure out how I feel about any of this. I have to work on the trial and keep them safe. No one is going to hurt them again.

Chapter Ten

Brittany

In less than seventy-two hours I've been arrested, spent the night in jail, been reunited with the love of my life and found out my daughter has known about him for a long time. I can't be too upset over the first two since they are the reason Casey is here now.

He's not the boy I left behind. His muscles have filled out and the stubble on his chin gives him that sexy edge he didn't have as a teenager. The kids are immediately enthralled with him as well. The drive to the hotel is full of questions from everyone. I sit quietly and take it all in, struggling to hold back tears. I'm awed by how easily he is accepting Austin, treating him no differently than he is Kacee.

He tells them all about their grandparents and how excited they are going to be to meet them. My stomach twists thinking of the reunion. They hated me all those years ago, and now that they know I kept their grandchild from them, they will likely despise me.

I'm pulled from my miserable thoughts when we pull up to the hotel and our doors are opened by valets. The kids look at me quizzically; I chuckle and tell them to grab their stuff and get out. My meager income has never allowed me to take them anywhere near this fancy, their dad's side of the family will quickly spoil them to luxuries I could never give them.

Casey passes money to the valet once the cart is loaded. I shiver when his hand lands gently on my lower back. I can feel the heat through my sweater.

"Should we get some dinner before heading up to the room?"

"Sure, but I insist on paying our part of the bill."

"Absolutely not, tonight we are celebrating. Plus, you have paid for everything for the last fifteen years. Let me take a turn."

I nod and look away, trying to hide my relief. The hotel restaurant is decadent to say the least, I'm not sure how many meals I could have managed here.

The kids can barely contain their excitement as their chairs are pulled out for them, and Austin giggles when the waiter lays his napkin across his lap. We order drinks and Casey orders a couple of appetizers. My mouth waters while reading the menu. I haven't had lobster in a very long time, not to mention a perfectly cooked steak.

"So kids, is your mother as good of a cook as I remember?"

I cock an eyebrow at him over my menu and we both laugh at the look of horror on both kids' faces.

"Mom, you used to be able to cook? What happened?"

"Very funny, Austin."

"Actually, Kacee takes after you and is quite good in the kitchen, she masters pretty much every recipe she tries. I think she learned out of desperation to keep me away."

"Of course not, Mom." She ruins this declaration by nodding her head yes to her dad.

"Is everyone ready to order?"

"Okay, guys, we're celebrating our reunion so order whatever you want." He leans over and whispers in my ear. "I know how much you like to eat so don't even think about ordering the cheapest thing on the menu."

After his cheap shot about my cooking, it serves him right to treat me to a big dinner. Steak and lobster it is; I slap the menu closed with a definitive nod of my head.

After everyone orders, awkward silence ensues, but luckily Casey is a born talker and quickly fills the gap.

"So Kacee, tell me about school, what grade are you in? Have you started thinking about college?"

I sit back contentedly and listen as she tells him all about eleventh grade and all her extracurricular activities. For a brief minute I let myself get excited about all of this.

"It sounds like you have a lot going on so why were you at a place like The Haunt, and on a school night no less?"

His judging tone rankles me instantly. Kacee looks to me to answer.

"If you would like to discuss my parenting decisions perhaps we can do that later?"

"You're right, I'm sorry. I can see you have done a great job and didn't mean to sound harsh."

He turns to Austin, asking him how elementary school has been treating him. Kacee is chewing on a roll looking miserable, having two parents is going to be an adjustment for all of us.

While Austin regales us with tales of his first grade adventure, we enjoy salads and dig into our entrees.

Half way through the meal, I feel his hand squeeze my knee as he leans toward me. "Do you realize you are moaning every time you take a bite? It's quiet but it's definitely coming from you."

I choke on the bite I was trying to swallow. How mortifying. "I guess it's been awhile since I've had a good piece of meat."

Now it's his turn to make a choking sound. Score one for me.

The rest of the meal passes peacefully. We order two desserts and share them between us.

"Okay, guys, let's get upstairs and get settled in. You still have school tomorrow."

All three of them give me sad puppy dog faces. Just what I need, another child. "Don't give me those looks; you only have two more days before the weekend, then you can play together all you want.”

“What time do we need to get up to get everyone to school?”

“I’ll need to get Kacee up at 5:30 if we’re going to drive to school.”

“Ugh, I forgot how early high school is.”

“Lucky for me she usually gets herself up and off to the bus stop so I can sleep a little later.”

“If you want to take a break, I don’t mind taking her in while you guys are staying here. It will give me more time to get to know her, too. I’ll grab some donuts on the way back then take Austin to school and you to work before going into the precinct for a bit.”

I look to Kacee to see what she thinks and she gives me a small nod and smiles.

“Sounds like we have a plan.”

Chapter Eleven

Casey

The knock on my bedroom door pulls me from my thoughts, not that they were anything exciting. I was lying in bed contemplating the family sharing a suite with me. Kacee is amazing and I can see so much of myself in her. I was wrong to make that jab at Brittany, she has obviously done a great job raising her. Austin is hysterical and has a huge heart, I can't understand why his father wouldn't want to see him. Some bastards don't deserve to be fathers.

Then of course there is Brittany, she is as beautiful as ever and I ache for her as much as I did when we were kids. That's a lie, I want her more now. Her body has filled out in ways only a mother's does and my hands itch to touch her. Her soft moans while she ate drove me to distraction. Thank god for my jacket or things would have gotten really embarrassing when we stood up to leave.

I grab a shirt in case it's one of the kids and I can't stop the smile when I open the door to a nervous looking Brittany. I drop the shirt behind the door and open it wide. As hoped, I hear her breath hitch and her eyes drop to study my chest and stomach. I may not have huge, bulging muscles but my six-pack will hopefully be enough to tempt her.

She bites her lip when she gets to the happy trail disappearing into my pajama pants, that was always one of her favorite parts.

"Are you guys settled in okay?"

"Oh, um yeah, the kids are showered and in bed." She smiles and holds out a rather large book, "I packed Kacee's baby album, I thought you might want to see it."

I instantly sober. Here I am trying to tease her and she is bringing me something important. I grab it and rush over to the couch. I sit and see she is still standing in the doorway.

"You can come in; I want to hear all the stories behind these pictures."

I move the book between us and open the cover. My breath is taken away by the pale sixteen-year-old Brittany in various pictures holding her ever growing belly.

"Grandma insisted on taking pictures throughout the pregnancy. She swore one day I would be glad she did. I hate to admit it but I will always be grateful for everything she and my mom did for me. I'm embarrassed to say there were days I would lay in bed and cry. I cried for you, for me, for the little girl who wouldn't know you. Then she would move inside me and I would remember I needed to be strong for her so I picked myself up and kept going. Not that Grandma gave me much choice. Even when my due date came, she still had me at the table working on my GED."

I shake my head, frustrated already, "I don't want there to be bitter or resentful feelings inside me, but I admit they are there. I should have been there helping you get through this. You shouldn't have been the only one who's life had to change, you must resent me for continuing on."

"No, not at all." She grabs my hand and turns pleading eyes to me, "We left so you could have everything you deserve. I admit in the beginning I didn't agree with my mom. We would get into screaming matches and she would actually unplug and take the house phone with her so I couldn't call you. It wasn't till my first day of school here that I finally got it. People treated me like a pariah, I only lasted a week before I begged her to let me take the GED test instead. I was so miserable in the beginning, I'm glad you didn't have to go through all of that."

Tears fill my eyes as the pictures progress through the labor. Her mom is there wiping sweat off her forehead, Grandma's in the picture holding her hand through a contraction. I stop flipping through the book and bring it closer to my face.

"Is that our prom picture?"

"Yep, you were my focal point during the contractions. It was the next best thing to having you there with me."

"How did it happen?"

"Well, my due date had come and gone and the doctors were considering inducing labor if it didn't happen soon. Grandma and Mom spent every free minute walking me around the neighborhood and the park. Some days I felt like a work horse, they were relentless in their pace and kept making me go. After five days of this I was ready to give up, nothing was happening. Finally, that fifth night I was in the bathroom brushing my teeth when I suddenly felt liquid running down my legs. At first I thought it was pee and didn't really think anything of it till the pain started."

She laughed at the memory and her whole face lit up. The sight took my breath away.

"I had imagined the pain would start small and build up but, it felt like I was being stabbed in the lower back from the get go. Everyone came running and they actually laughed at me when the next scream came. Apparently my pain was their pleasure. Mom called the doctor, who said he wanted me to come in when the contractions were steadily ten minutes apart. Since I was so young, he didn't want to take any chances of complications developing before I got there. The first couple of hours I spent mostly kneeling backwards on the couch while they took turns massaging my back. Finally, just after two a.m. we decided it was time to go in. Once I was admitted, they hooked me up and as soon as I could, I got the epidural. It became easier for a while and I was actually able to snooze for a couple of hours. I think they had the epidural too high because when they finally turned it down and told me to push, a lot of pain came back."

"Oh god, what is that?" My gag reflex was in full working order.

"Oh, I'm sorry, I forgot that was in there. I told you Grandma insisted on documenting everything. That's Kacee's head coming out."

"I didn't know it was such a bloody process."

"I don't know what a normal amount is but the doctors didn't seem to be worried," she flipped the page and I couldn't hold back the gagging noise, "and that is the placenta. Why she felt the need to take a picture of that coming out I will never know."

"I could have gone my whole life without needing to see that. Thank god I don't eat my steak rare or I probably would be abstaining for a while."

She laughs and flips the page again. "And here is where your perfect seven-pound, three-ounce daughter came wailing into the world at 6:53 a.m."

"Holy cow, look at that cone head!"

"Yeah, that scared me at first but they assured me it would fix itself."

My finger strokes the picture of a sweaty Brittany smiling as she hugs our baby. Words are robbed from me; I've missed so much. Her hand gently rests on my shoulder, it takes a minute before I can look up at her.

"You made a beautiful baby, I was so thankful she came out looking like you."

The book slid from our laps when I grab her into a bone crushing hug, forgetting for a minute that we haven't seen each other in fifteen years. I am completely overwhelmed by my awe for everything she has been through. I want more than anything to open my eyes and be sixteen again. We deserve a do over to that weekend. I want to be a scared kid worrying what we were going to do with a newborn baby.

I open one eye then the other, disappointment clearly written on my face to see my wish hadn't come true. I clear my throat and pull away awkwardly.

"Do you have any more books?"

She picks up the album from the floor and chuckles. "I have shelves full of albums and quite a few VHS tapes if you still happen to have a VCR packed away?"

"Oh my god, a VCR, I haven't thought of one of those in a while. I'll have to see what I can find." I couldn't help chuckling at the idea of asking my assistant to hunt one down for me.

"Tomorrow after work, I'll stop at the apartment and get everything."

"I'll go with you to make sure nobody's sitting outside again. Now, let's finish this book."

Three hours later, our eyes are blurry and we can't hold back the yawns any longer. It's almost three a.m. and we have to get Kacee up in a couple of hours. The book finished after Kacee's first birthday. We laughed, we cried, and my anger melted a little bit each hour.

Chapter Twelve

Brittany

The smell of bacon wakes me up first, then the sound of Austin's giggles brings me fully awake.

"You were right, waving the bacon by her face did the trick! I think she's coming to."

I peek out from one eye to see Casey and Austin standing over me with stupid grins on their faces. What must I look like? I definitely feel drool on my chin. You know what, who cares. He kept me up that late, he can see the harsh reality of what I look like in the mornings.

"You're lucky you brought food or I wouldn't be so nice about being woken up."

"Come on, Mommy, we also got you crappies and hot tea."

"I appreciate the offer but I don't want any crap for breakfast."

"Don't worry, you're safe. We ordered crepes. I let him pick the food off the menu."

I grab Austin and snuggle him against me, "Should I be worried you picked crappies for me?"

His infectious giggles have everyone laughing.

"Casey, help me, she's attacking me!"

I hold on long enough to let Austin feel like he's being rescued before letting go.

"I promise there was a picture and he was not intentionally picking poop."

"Okay, I'll believe you this time. Is Kacee ready to go?"

"Actually, I took her to school a while ago. I got Austin ready and as soon as you are dressed, we'll drop him off then get you to work."

I grab my phone and see it's eight o'clock and my alarms were shut off.

"I wanted to let you sleep in as long as you could. Kacee shut them off so you wouldn't be disturbed."

"That was very sweet of you, I appreciate the gesture."

"Plus I remember how grumpy you used to be when you didn't get much sleep."

"Gesture ruined." I chuck my pillow at him, trying to hide my smile. "Now get out and let me get ready."

Once they are gone, I flop back on my pillow with a deep sigh. Is Casey Sanders really here? How many years did I dream this wasn't real and I had stayed with him? I pinch myself to make sure I really am awake. Yep, that hurt, this is real. Austin's giggles from the living room remind me I need to get moving and with one last big stretch, I shuffle off to the bathroom.

The fluorescent lighting blinds me momentarily till I find my reflection. Ugh, he really did wake the dragon this morning, didn't he? It's been years since I've stayed up that late, so much for looking like Sleeping Beauty. The bags under my eyes remind me I'm no spring chicken anymore and he has a gorgeous fiancée back home who probably has a perfect body like he does. I throw the washcloth at myself in the mirror and turn to the shower. I need to stop caring; he'll be back in his world as soon as my case is closed.

After a quick shower where I desperately try to forget his tan stomach and muscled shoulders when he hugged me last night, it took a lot of effort not to try out the extendable shower head. I need to keep thinking of the beauty waiting for him back home to cool me down.

Getting dressed between bites of breakfast, I refuse to acknowledge to myself that I'm spending more time on my hair and makeup than I have done in years. It's easier to lie and say I need to put on a good show around town while I'm waiting on my trial.

"Mom, come on, I'm going to be late."

With one last look in the mirror, I give myself a confident nod and head out to the living room separating our bedrooms.

"Okay, okay, hold your horses, I'm ready." I pause to glare at them, they are sprawled across the couches pretending to be asleep. "Really, guys? I didn't take that long."

With a loud snore from Casey, he pretends to jerk awake and shake Austin awake, too.

"Hurry, Austin, to the bat mobile before she starts doing something else. Lucky for us I called ahead to have the valet pull the car up."

In an impressively manly gesture, he grabs Austin and throws him over his shoulder like a sack of potatoes, grabs his backpack and stands up effortlessly. I may need to change my underwear already.

Realizing my mouth is open and I'm staring, I clear my throat and head for the door quickly. This arrangement is going to be torture. To make matters worse, I'm sharing a room with my kids so I can't even get a little me time with Casey starring in my fantasy.

Casey sits Austin down when the elevator comes and lets him push the buttons.

"Austin mentioned he buys school lunch so I didn't need to worry about packing anything for him. I'm not sure what you normally do for lunch but if you would like, I can swing by and we can grab something near your work?"

"That should be fine. Oh crap, Kacee is going to need a ride, too. Normally she buses to the apartment."

"Don't worry, it's all covered. I told her I would pick her up from school. I thought it would give us a chance to hang out more, then we'll pick up Austin and you later."

"You are efficient, aren't you?"

"My secretary would disagree. She will tell you I couldn't survive a day without her and she's right. I guess she has rubbed off on me a little. Don't tell her though, it will make her smug."

I chuckle and smile at the doorman who holds the car door open.

After a short drive, we drop Austin at school and within another few minutes, we're at my building.

"So if you'll text me when you are on your way, I'll be ready down here then we can go to the cafe down the street."

"Sounds like a plan, have a good day at work."

With an awkward smile, I jump out and head into work. My dreams are finally a reality, even though they will be short lived, and to think, it only took getting arrested for it to happen.

Chapter Thirteen

Casey

I need to focus on Brittany's case but that album threw me for a loop. It's not that I haven't thought about having kids. I think deep down I knew Monica wasn't right for me and that's what's been holding me back from setting a wedding date and starting our family. Seeing Brittany like I remember her but holding our baby was possibly the most overwhelming experience of my life. How can I go back to my old life now?

I open the precinct door and feel a hand slap me on the back.

"Earth to Casey, I called your name five times. You are seriously in your own head, aren't you?"

"Oh sorry, Carter, I was thinking about the case."

"More like thinking about the woman involved in the case. You guys seem to have some serious history."

I hear the curiosity in his voice as much as the concern. We're all taught not to handle cases that are personal to us. I'm only allowed to help as long as he lets me, he can't know how close I am to all of this.

"I haven't seen Brittany in a long time so it was a bit of a shock to catch up. Now how about we start looking through those witness statements?"

I walk on before he can say anything further. We head back to the arresting officer's desk, so far everyone has been very polite. If there are any cops who are friendly with the Montgomery's, they have really good poker faces.

"Hey, Steve, do you have the rest of the statements ready for us to read over?"

He stands and shakes our hands firmly.

"I've got everything in the conference room over there." He walks into the room and waves us in, then looks out in the hall before speaking again, "I really don't want that douche bag getting away with this so if you guys need anything, let me know. I can help on my time off, too, if you think I can be of any use."

He hands us his card; his cell number is circled in the bottom corner.

"I'll leave you guys to it then. Oh and there's fresh coffee in the break room if you need some."

"Thanks, Steve, and I'm sure we'll be in touch."

I wait till the door is closed before turning back to Carter.

"So is he someone we can trust or is he staying close to keep tabs?"

"I don't know exactly who we can trust but as far as I know, he's always been a good guy. How about we be careful what we share with him?"

With a quick nod, I sit down and grab the first file off the stack.

Two hours later, I can't control my frustration any longer and slap down the file in my hand.

"Are you kidding me? These statements are ridiculous. Everyone has the exact same story and they all claim Kacee was never there and Brittany was unprovoked in her attack."

"All the ones I've read say the same thing. I told you this wasn't going to be easy."

"Do we know if there were any surveillance cameras in there? And why the hell did they let a minor in that place anyway?"

He grabs another file and flips through for a minute.

"Says here the cameras were off that night so they didn't get any of this on tape. We can't get the owner on the minor thing either because they do teen night once a week, anyone fourteen to twenty can be in there.”

“There has to be someone who is willing to tell the truth.” I can’t hide the slight edge of desperation in my voice.

“Why don’t you go get some lunch then we’ll work on the paperwork to get a change of venue. If we can get it moved out of the area, she has a good shot at a fair trial.”

“Maybe I can make some calls and see if anyone has a connection out here. We have to get that venue change approved. I won’t lose this case.”

Chapter Fourteen

Brittany

"Spill the beans, what haven't you been telling me?"

I look up from my computer and stare wide-eyed at Sharon. I wasn't ready to tell everyone about the case yet but apparently my best friend of five years knows.

"I was going to tell you, I swear."

"Seriously, how can you keep such a delicious secret from me?"

Um, now I'm confused. I raise my eyebrow and wait for her to go on. No reason to spill more than I need to.

"The guy...in the reception area asking for you? He said you are expecting him?"

I look at the clock and see it's a quarter to twelve. He's early and he was supposed to text me to come down. So much for keeping things to myself for a while.

"Oh, you mean Mr. Sanders. Well, he's actually here on business but we're going to discuss it over lunch."

I can see the skepticism in her eyes. After all, I'm an office assistant, what kind of business do I need to attend to? No reason to tell her it's personal yet.

"If he's available, you better turn that business into pleasure soon. It's been a while for you and you could use the release."

I give her a mocking shocked face before giggling and walking out to reception. She catches up easily and follows me out. She's determined to embarrass me, I know it.

Coming around the corner, I see him standing by the window staring out at the city. God, he is gorgeous. When will this punch to the gut feeling stop?

"Casey, all set?"

I hear Sharon clear her throat, of course she wants an introduction.

"This is my friend, Sharon; Sharon, this is Casey Sanders."

"How funny, you have the same first name as her daughter."

My eyes bulge and his baby blues flicker to my face and back to hers.

"That is an interesting coincidence, isn't it?"

"Well, I only get forty-five minutes for lunch so we best get going."

"Have fun, I'll be here when you get back."

I glare at her over my shoulder as I follow him out the door. I can expect an interrogation when I get back.

Being the perfect gentleman, he opens all the doors for me, pulls my chair out and lets me order first. It's refreshing to be with someone who has manners. Joey, my ex, was not such a catch after all.

I'm pulled from my musings when the waiter returns with our salads.

"So how's everything going with Mr. Carter so far? Have you guys made much progress?"

"I'll be honest, we have an uphill battle ahead of us, but he's a sharp guy and knows the locals so we should be able to get this taken care of quickly. If I can get proof against Dirk, I think we can pressure him to drop the case."

"But being who he is, I'm guessing you aren't finding anyone to speak up against him?"

The worry in my stomach returns. As much as I want to believe Casey is my knight in shining armor and can rescue me, I am a realist and know who we're dealing with.

"We're still combing through everything, but let's talk about something else. How about telling me about what happened to you after your GED? Have you been at this job the entire time?"

I can't help the smile at seeing his genuine curiosity.

"Actually, I was able to stay home with Kacee until she was two, but then Mom wanted to move out of Grandma's place so I got a part-time job at the same restaurant Mom was working at. The owners were cool, they made sure to never schedule us at the same time. I still pick up shifts there when I can. That's where I was when Kacee called the other night. After Austin's dad left, the kids and I had to move in with Mom for a while. She would have been happy if we had stayed forever, but I wanted my own place. So I got this assistant job and after a year, I was able to give the kids an apartment with their own rooms."

He reaches for my hand across the table, the pain evident in his eyes.

"I am so sorry you have had to work two jobs and do this on your own. You never wanted that life for your mother and I sure as hell don't want it for you now."

I pull my hand away, perturbed at his audacity to make it seem like I have been suffering without him.

"I appreciate that but if you think about it, I am doing really well for a girl with a GED and no college degree. Did I have regrets, moments of anger? Sure, that's what makes me human. The way I look at it, I never would have had those two beautiful children if I hadn't gone down this path."

"Beautifully said. I didn't mean to imply you had a bad life." His sheepish look soothes my irritation.

"No offense taken. Now, tell me about your fiancée."

The fork stops halfway to his mouth; let's see how he likes the spotlight being on him instead.

"Well, we met at a charity event about six years ago. She works for the Mayor's office and hopes to run for office one day herself."

"She sounds ambitious," and way classier than me. "When's the wedding?"

"We haven't set a date yet." He has the good sense to look sheepish.

"Wait, I read that you have been engaged to her for a few years."

"You read that? Have you been checking up on me?"

I feel the blush immediately; I hadn't meant to give that away. "No, maybe Kacee mentioned it?"

"Come on, admit it, you Googled me."

"I may have looked you up while I was at work this morning. I was curious."

That warm, strong hand reaches across the table for my hand again. God, he needs to stop touching me or it's going to really be a struggle to keep my hands off him.

"You can ask me anything, you don't need to read articles."

"Okay, why haven't you married her yet? Most women would not tolerate such a long engagement." I bite my lip, desperate to know the answer and desperate to not hear it.

"It hasn't felt right. We aren't a perfect love match and she knows that. I'm sure part of her reason for staying is because I am likely the next District Attorney. Not to say she is using me, I know she loves me. She has been pushing for a date from the beginning and that was when I was still a newly hired lawyer at the bottom of the food chain."

I hate to admit his answer sparked hope deep inside me. If they aren't a love match, do I still have a chance with him?

"Well, I guess it's time to get you back to the office, plus I have another date to get to. I was thinking of taking Kacee out for ice cream, do you think she will like that? I mean I know she's fifteen but they still like ice cream at that age, right?"

The slightly panicked look in his eyes is endearing. "Stop worrying so much, she already loves you. Be yourself and everything will happen naturally."

"You're right, I got this."

I think he's saying that more for his benefit than mine.

We walk the short distance back to my office and stand awkwardly at the entrance. What is the proper goodbye in this case?

"I guess I better get inside. You'll pick up Austin at three and be back here at five for me?"

"Yes, ma'am."

He gives me a mock salute and a cheeky grin before heading to the parking garage for his car. Part of me wants him by my side so he can't leave but damn, it's a nice sight to see.

Chapter Fifteen

Casey

Am I seriously sitting in a car line waiting to pick up my daughter? It's surreal to think this person that is half me has been walking around and I had no idea of her existence. My cell phone vibrating in the cup holder distracts me from searching her out in the crowd. With a resigned sigh, I hit the hands-free button and hear my mother's voice come over the car speakers.

"Casey, is everything all right? I called the office and your assistant said you've taken a few days off. I called Monica and she said you flew out for an emergency. How can you take off without letting us know? I was so worried."

She finally takes a breath long enough for me to cut in. "Everything's fine, an old friend called and said they needed help. I'm in Utah for a little while, I'll be home as soon as this is wrapped up."

I stare expectantly at the dashboard, confused as to why there is silence. She never lets there be silence.

"Mom, are you there?"

"Oh, yes dear, something distracted me. I have to run, let me know when you are coming home."

Without a love you or goodbye, she hangs up. I have never gotten off the phone with her in less than thirty minutes. A knock on the passenger window distracts me. My breath is taken away by Kacee's beautiful face smiling in at me. It's still a shock to see her. With the exception of her eyes and hair, she is the spitting image of her mother. I hit the unlock button and wave her in.

"Hi, Dad."

That is so weird to hear, it's probably best to play it cool. "Hi, how was your day?"

"Okay, there's a lot of rumors going around about what happened at the club the other night but nothing I can't handle. I got a B on my chemistry exam," she waves the papers at me. "So, what are we going to do till Austin gets out?"

The changes in subjects almost give me whiplash. I'm relieved she is handling rumors so well. I glance at the papers from one of my most hated subjects in school.

"If you are up for it, I thought we'd go get some ice cream and catch up?"

"Sounds good, we can go to Hannagan's a couple of blocks over, they are the best."

I punch the name in my GPS and take off. "I was thinking we could play a version of twenty questions to get to know each other, are you up for it?"

"Sounds fun, I'll start. Star Trek or Star Wars?"

I like that her mind goes to geekdom first, that's promising. "Star Wars for sure."

"Oh thank god, I was really hoping you were a cool dad."

We laugh but now I'm nervous. This suddenly feels more like a job interview. Maybe this was a bad idea.

"Reading or video games?"

"I never really had time for video games, I went from high school to college to law school to the law firm. I like reading when I have time though."

"That's the saddest answer I've ever heard." I look over at her crestfallen face, she actually looks sad for me.

"What's that look for?"

"Did you have any fun growing up?"

"Of course I did. Actually the year with your mother was the best but I had other fun, too."

"Will you tell me about her, the girl she was in high school?"

"Of course, but first I have a very important question for you-chocolate or vanilla?"

"Neither, cookie dough."

"Ooh, nice. I'm a chocolate brownie guy myself but I can respect cookie dough. Let's order then I'll tell you about your mom."

After a short wait, we get our ice cream cones and sit in a booth.

"Okay, spill the beans. I want to hear about her."

"She saved me from a life of loneliness. Your grandparents are very serious people; they have always had high expectations for me. I spent a lot of time studying or with tutors, and they always pushed me to be the best. I didn't make friends easily so you can imagine my surprise when your mom sat down at my lunch table and started talking to me at the end of our sophomore year." The ice cream melting down my fingers is momentarily forgotten as I think back to that day for the thousandth time.

"She said she had heard I was fluent in Spanish and she was wondering if I could tutor her. At first I looked like a complete idiot staring at her. I was awestruck by her and couldn't find any words. After a minute, I finally found my tongue and managed to squeak out a yes. We agreed to meet in the library after school. In my dorky hastiness, I ran right to Señora Vasquez, the Spanish teacher, to find out what I should be helping Brittany with. Imagine my surprise when she tells me she doesn't know why Brittany needs a tutor. She was top student in the class and ahead of most of the other kids. As you can imagine, I thought she was playing some kind of prank on me." I pause to lick the dripping ice cream and get it back under control. Kacee is leaning forward, impatiently waiting for me to continue.

"Angry at myself for getting my hopes up, and angry at her for jerking me around, I stormed into the library and demanded to know what her game was. I'll never forget her wide-eyed stare, the blush creeping across her cheeks making the caramel brown of her eyes stand out even more. Her words stole my breath and made me fall into the chair across from her. She said she thought I was cute and wanted to get to know me. She also knew I was number one in our class and a loner so she made up the excuse to get to know me."

Kacee slumps back against the booth, laughing uncontrollably. With one eyebrow quirked, I wait for her to finish her obvious enjoyment of my awkward youth.

"I'm sorry, I'm trying to picture Mom's face when you caught her and she had to admit the truth. That is a nightmare for any girl, let alone Mom who is so shy and introverted."

"That's where you are wrong, there was nothing timid about her. I had watched her from the first day of high school. She was friendly to everyone and people loved her. Well, everyone except your grandparents. They thought I deserved someone better than her. I think they were wrong; I was never good enough for her."

The smile fades from my face as I think back on all the times my parents treated her poorly. No wonder they took off when they found out about the pregnancy. They knew my family was never going to accept it. My parents are as much to blame for us being in this situation as we are. All that anger I had at them years ago bubbles back up.

"Earth to Dad, I think I lost you there."

"I'm sorry, I got stuck in the past for a minute." The alarm on my phone beeps, alerting me it's time to get Austin. "Well, that's enough reminiscing for today. Let's go get your brother."

Chapter Sixteen

Brittany

The end of a work day has never come slower before; I can't concentrate on work knowing Casey is picking me up soon. It took everything I had not to sigh and giggle when I was interrogated by Sharon after lunch. I'm trying to be realistic, I know he is going home soon, but I can't help it. I've never stopped loving him and now he's here, in the flesh and looking so much better than in my dreams.

Second by second, the minute's tick by till it's finally five o'clock. I've never packed up so fast in my life. With a wave to my boss, I rush to the elevator to find Sharon waiting patiently for me.

"Oh good, I caught you, I thought we could walk to the train together."

"Actually, I will be getting a ride for the next few days."

Her smile widens, "Just as I thought."

The elevator doors close behind us and I'm trapped. She's acting innocent but I know she's dying to see who's picking me up. She acts like I've never dated before...technically I haven't in all the years I've known her so she's not completely off base.

We exit the building and come face to face with my family, and the sight is beautiful. Austin is sitting on the trunk of Casey's car while the other two huddle around him. They are intently playing something on their cell phones and I can hear them egging each other on. Sharon sticks by me as we walk up and interrupt the fun.

"Am I interrupting?"

"Oh hi, Britt, this round is almost over, give us a few more seconds." His eyebrows are drawn together, intently focused on the game. All at once there is shouting as Casey throws his hands in the air claiming to be the champion. Is he really gloating that he beat two kids?

"Hey, Mom, did you know Dad has never played a video game before? I checked his phone, there wasn't one fun app on there."

I hear Sharon's gasp. Shit, she heard Kacee say Dad. So much for keeping this low key for a while.

"Okay everyone, say bye to Sharon and let's get home." That little bomb is going to drive her crazy all night. I smile at her as Casey holds my door open for me. I'm evil, I know.

"Did everyone have a good day? I'm glad to see you all survived the afternoon together."

Both kids start talking at the same time, excited to say what they did with their new hero. Have they really been starved for male attention? Sitting back, I relax as they take turns recounting every conversation I missed.

"Dad says you were quite the hottie in high school."

Austin giggles and I can't hide my shock as I look at Casey, who has the good sense to look embarrassed. I'm not sure I want him regaling the kids with my high school exploits. His electric blue eyes bore into mine, "I still think you are." His barely whispered words send tingles straight to my lady parts. He did not just say that. I glance back. The kids apparently didn't hear him, maybe it was wishful thinking.

"Okay, we're here. Grab anything else you may need then we'll head back to the hotel."

The apartment building comes into view. I promised more baby memories, I hope he's ready for this. While the kids collect a few random items, I grab a large box out of the hall closet and set it on the kitchen table. After three more trips, I've filled a duffel bag with multiple photo albums.

"I hope you were serious about the albums because I have a ton of pictures and videos."

He whistles as he looks in the box, "You weren't kidding, were you? It's a good thing I'm here for a while."

After flinging the duffel across his back, he hoists the box and nods before heading downstairs. Showoff. The kids follow behind with bags in hand as I lock up, not knowing when we'll be back.

The drive to the hotel is animated and carefree. For a few minutes I get a glimpse into how life might have been had I stayed all those years ago.

"I was thinking an early dinner then homework then movie time. The hotel was going to have a VCR delivered to our room today."

"Sure, that sounds fun. It's been a while since I watched the tapes."

"Great, I'm going to follow the bell hop up to our room to drop all this stuff off. Why don't you guys get a table and order an appetizer."

I follow a very excited Austin and Kacee into the restaurant. They are definitely enjoying our new arrangement.

"Good evening, Mrs. Sanders, will your husband be joining you for dinner?"

The kids look at me with laughter in their eyes. If only the hostess knew how badly I wish Casey was my husband. "Yes, he'll be down in a few minutes."

I shrug at the kids and follow her to a table in the back corner. Once we're settled in and drinks are ordered, I finally get up the nerve to get serious with the kids.

"So guys, what do you really think of Casey? Is all of this okay?"

"He is awesome!"

"Austin's right, he is so much better than the guy I've been picturing in my head for the last year. I can see why you fell in love with him, he's perfect for you."

The look of adoration on their faces is more heartbreaking than anything else. I'm afraid they're getting too attached. "You guys do know he's going to have to go home soon, right? He has a job and a fiancée back home." Their crestfallen faces make me instantly regret saying anything. Am I trying to convince them or me? "I'm sure he's going to want to set up some kind of visitation schedule and you have another set of grandparents to spoil you, too."

"No offense, Mom, but if they don't like you, I don't want anything to do with them."

Kacee's loyalty is admirable. "Don't judge them too harshly. They were only trying to do what was best for your dad. Just because they are adults doesn't mean they are perfect, we all make mistakes."

Before we can say anymore, I see Casey heading toward us. Changing the subject, I distract the kids by talking about the menu.

"Sorry for the holdup, guys, my secretary called and needed me to work out some issues with my other cases."

"I didn't even think about that; I feel terrible taking you away from other people who need your help, too. If you need to head home, I'm sure Mr. Jepsen can handle everything here."

His strong hand covers mine and squeezes till I look up at him. "I am not going anywhere. You need me and I want to be here. Plus, what's the point of being a partner in a law firm if I can't delegate work? It's not like anyone can complain, I don't think I have taken a single sick day since I started there."

His beautiful electric blue eyes boring into mine send a shiver down my spine. I want to believe he isn't sticking around because of Kacee. I so badly want him to say he's here for me, too.

"Now let's eat up, there is a whole box of videos upstairs that we need to watch."

With the spell broken, I sigh and turn my attention back to my menu. Maybe I'll drown my feelings in a big bowl of pasta.

85

Chapter Seventeen

Casey

Sitting at dinner with Brittany and the kids, laughing and telling stories, is the most alive I have felt, well, probably since Brittany left. I realize now I've been living on autopilot, doing what was expected of me and going with the flow. That isn't really fair to me or Monica. I seriously need to make some changes in my life.

"Dad, we're almost done with homework, ten-minute warning till movie time." Hearing Kacee's bellow from the living room has me shaking my head. I am grateful that she has taken to me so easily, being a teenager is hard enough without adding in a new parent. I can't wait for Mom and Dad to meet her; they are going to love her.

The phone ringing on the desk distracts me, Monica's smiling face is staring up at me from the screen. Other than a few texts, I haven't really talked to her. I really don't want to break the news of a secret child over the phone.

"Hello?"

"Hey, sweetie, how's it going?"

"Everything's good here, the case is tougher than I thought it would be so I'm not sure how long this is going to take. The lawyer I'm working with seems like a good guy, though, and we're working on getting the case moved out of the area so hopefully we'll catch a break."

"It sounds like your friend is lucky to have you there helping. Do you need me to send anything out there, some more clothes maybe?"

Of course she would be the ever loving and helpful fiancée. It actually makes me feel guilty. "More clothes would be great, and thanks for understanding."

"Hey, I get it, but you may want to call your mom, she's been acting kind of weird. She keeps asking if we've talked and how you are doing."

"I'm starting to think she doesn't realize the umbilical cord was cut many years ago."

"You can't fault a mom for worrying. I'll let you go, I miss you and I love you."

"I love you too, and I'll talk to you soon. Bye."

With a guilt laden sigh, I toss the phone on the bed. Out of the corner of my eye I see someone in the doorway. Brittany's head is poking around the door and she gives me a shy smile.

"Sorry to intrude, the kids are getting their PJs on and we're ready to start the movies." Nibbling on her bottom lip, she glances at the phone. I assume she heard me say I love you, this couldn't get more awkward.

"Sounds good, I'll be there in a minute."

Changing out of my suit, I put on a t-shirt and sweatpants before joining them on the couches. "This is exciting; I feel like we should have popcorn or something." Austin's cheer of agreement has everyone laughing.

"Good idea, we're not going to get through all the movies tonight so we'll remember that for next time."

Brittany hits play then cuddles up with Austin. The first image to come up is a sixteen-year-old Brittany with messy hair who's trying to smile while she's grimacing. I recognize Maria's voice as she laughs and narrates what is happening.

"Well, it's after one a.m. and Brittany is having pretty intense back labor. Grandma is grabbing her bags because we're on our way to the hospital, baby Kacee is ready to come out. How are you feeling, Britt?"

"Like I want to punch Casey in his balls."

The camera spins around to a smiling Maria, "That's just the contractions talking, no harm will come to anyone's balls tonight."

Austin giggles and I turn a horrified face to Brittany. "What can I say, I was in pain."

"Car's ready, let's go have a baby."

I glance back at the T.V. and recognize Britt's grandmother from pictures that were up around her apartment. This smiling woman is the person who has been hiding my letters all these years. The anger bubbling up surprises me.

The video cuts over to Brittany relaxing in a hospital bed looking much better than she did before.

"We're all settled in and as you can tell, the epidural has been administered. I'm happy to say no one's genitals were harmed in the process."

"Ha-ha, very funny."

Everything around me disappears as I'm sucked in by her smiling face. It's exactly the way I remember her. This is my love, the girl who has haunted me all these years. I stare enthralled as the video progresses through labor, and I feel the tear slide down my cheek when they lay our daughter on Britt's exhausted chest. The next hour is various clips of firsts-her first bath, first time sitting up, first time eating from a spoon. All the while Brittany is growing up, too, her beauty continuing to evolve as she grows into motherhood.

The tape ends and the spell is broken. As the blood rushing in my ears quiets down, I hear Brittany whisper to Kacee to take Austin to bed with her. At some point during the movie I had leaned forward, elbows on my knees, my chin resting on fisted hands. The softest touch on my shoulder causes me to jump up, pain constricting my breathing.

"Are you okay?"

"I...I don't know what to say." Emotions I hadn't felt in a long time were threatening to explode out of me. Before I do anything rash, I take off for my room and go out on the balcony; maybe fresh air can calm me down.

After a few minutes, the ache in my chest starts easing and I'm mortified at my reaction. I asked to watch those tapes and then I freak out on them. The balcony door sliding open draws my attention. A nervous looking Brittany walks out with two glasses of wine.

"I thought we could both use this." She hands me the wine then sits on the chair across from me.

"I hope I didn't scare the kids?"

"Austin is oblivious and Kacee gets it. You were the last one to find out about all this, it can't be easy."

"I thought I had come to terms with this, I didn't expect to react that way. Seeing you exactly how I remember you but swollen with our child was the most intense pain I have ever felt. Well, that's not true, it's second to the day I found you gone." The more I talked, the angrier I felt. Turning anguished eyes to her, I can tell she's shocked at my words. "I spent years trying to get over you. Do you know people tried to get me to believe you were dead? I was a kid, no one would help me, the police wouldn't listen to me. You left me. You came here, started a new life and cut me out of it. How could you do that, how could you look that happy in those videos? You were stuck in my soul, I suffered without you. No one else loved me like you did. You...left...me."

"Saying I'm sorry isn't enough but it's all I have. We did what we thought was best and look, it all worked out. You are here now, with us."

"It all worked out? Really? You are on trial and our daughter was almost raped. If I had been in her life, she would have never even been allowed to go to that club. You did what you thought was best but maybe your best wasn't good enough."

I regret the words as soon as they are out but I can't take them back. I wanted her to hurt, to feel an ounce of the pain I was in.

I can see I have crushed her and I can't add that guilt right now. Setting down my wine glass, I head inside. I need to get away.

As soon as the valet gets my car, I peel out and leave them all behind me. Driving through the city with no destination in mind gives me time to calm down. As fate would have it, I stumble upon The Haunt, the nightclub that started all this drama. I can't hide the smile when I see Dirk's SUV parked in front. I have a pretty good idea of how to get rid of some of this excess rage.

The music blaring out the open door doesn't dim the noise from the crowd obviously having a good time inside. Lucky for me, it doesn't take long to find Dirk. It's no surprise to see him sitting on a couch with a girl on his lap and thugs all around him. I grab a beer from the bar and find the nearest high top in his sight and wait for him to spot me.

Maybe he can feel my anger pulsating toward him because it doesn't take long for him to see me. The smile drops from his face, he shoves the girl off him and stomps toward me. Not wanting him to get the upper hand, I sip on my drink with a bored look on my face.

"I'll give you credit, you have balls coming in here."

"I was curious to see the place where you tried to rape Kacee." I can tell he's shocked by my candid accusation.

"I don't know what you are referring to. I have never seen Kacee in here." His friends chuckle at his obvious lie. "Isn't it kind of late for you to be out, don't you have a whore to defend?"

"I know you think you are tough, hiding behind your daddy like you are untouchable, but I promise you, I will get you. Leave them alone or I will bury you and your entire family. I will make it my life's mission to uncover everything your family does and take it public. I'll laugh in your face as I watch your entire world collapse around you. Now be a good little boy and let your daddy know I'm not afraid of any of you."

The rage in his eyes is a soothing balm to my soul. With a smile and a wink, I walk out of the bar and drive back to my family.

Chapter Eighteen

Brittany

The alarm beeping on my phone drills through my brain. I never heard Casey come back last night. I tried to stay awake but I finally passed out around two a.m.

"Mom, go back to sleep for a while. Dad is going to drop me at school then come back for you guys."

My mind races with this information. He's here and he's not ignoring Kacee, that's a good sign. I get his anger; he has every right to feel betrayed. I was the only person who showed him any love and affection and I took off without warning. Those home movies were supposed to bring us closer, but instead I forced him to bare his soul and it was painful for both of us. I hope we can get past this.

"It's okay, sweetie, I'll take my time getting ready. Can you let him know Austin and I will be in the restaurant downstairs when he gets back?"

"Sure thing, love you, bye!" With a quick kiss on the cheek, she hurries out of the room. Glancing over I see Austin's tiny body still curled into a ball, blissfully unaware of the early hour. With a groan, I drag my tired butt off to shower, leaving the door cracked in case he wakes up.

The hot water seeping into my bones washes away my gloominess and helps energize me. I swear I'm part water goddess or something, water really does make me feel better. I definitely feel more confident to see Casey again.

With only a little bit of grumbling from Austin before he finally wakes up, it only takes bribing him with eating downstairs to have him finally pop up.

We grab our usual table and order waffles. As soon as the waiter is gone, I take advantage of our alone time to see how he is taking all these changes.

"So Casey seems pretty cool, what do you think of him?"

"He's awesome! He's just like I thought a daddy would be." The excitement in his eyes dulls, "Is he really going to leave soon?"

"Well, he has a job back home, he never meant to stay here forever."

"But if you tell him how much you are going to miss him, he'll stay." Am I that transparent that my child can tell I still love him? "Me and Kacee will miss him, too!" His tear-filled eyes break my heart. Before I can say more, I see the object of our discussion baring down on us. He ruffles Austin's hair before sitting down and noticing how miserable he looks.

"Hey buddy, what's going on? Why the sad face?"

Austin's eyes drop to his lap, "I don't want you to go home," he mumbles.

Great, now Casey knows we were talking about him. He looks to me and I shrug, what can I possibly say to that?

"Why are we worrying about that? I've already told you guys that you are going with me to meet your grandparents. Your mom and I will work something out. I'm not going anywhere kiddo, you're stuck with me."

Austin's wide toothy grin is a sign that the crisis has been averted.

"Now finish your food so we can get you to school."

It doesn't take long to scarf down our food and get on the road. I'm actually dreading dropping Austin off first, that means I'll be alone with Casey and that means we'll have to talk about last night.

After a quick kiss and a hug, Austin is in the school and the silence in the car is deafening. The car pulls out; I'm relaxed instantly, thinking we'll have a quiet ride to work. Instead he pulls over into a shady parking spot. The soft leather of his seats makes a rubbing noise as I see him turn toward me. Here we go.

"I want to apologize for my outburst last night. I had no right to say the things I did. I obviously am not as okay with this as much as I thought I was. I promise to keep my emotions in better check from now on. Please forgive me for the terrible things I said."

I don't realize my jaw has dropped until I try to swallow and realize my entire mouth has gone dry. Is he seriously apologizing to me? He really is a saint, isn't he?

"This is an incredibly stressful time for both of us. I have turned your life upside down and didn't take into account how you are handling this. I think we both have a long way to go before everything is okay again."

There, that sounded very grown up. What I really wanted to say was that we were stupid and wrong to leave him, I still love him and I want him back in my bed. Somehow I don't think that would have been the appropriate response though.

"I would like to keep watching those movies," I think he sees the panic in my eyes, "but don't worry, I'm better prepared this time and promise not to freak out again. I need to see them; I need to know everything I've missed. So many scenarios have played in my head since you left. Watching these tapes will help me come to terms with everything I have worried about for the last sixteen years."

A puzzled look crosses his face before turning into laughter. I stare questioningly at him, waiting for an explanation. "I'm sorry, I just realized it's over. All the therapy, shutting myself in for letter day, mourning your loss, it's all over. I actually feel free." The utter look of relief mixed with happiness lifts a weight off my shoulders I didn't realize was there till now. Maybe he's right, maybe we can both move on and be okay again.

"That's enough of the heavy stuff for today. Let's get you to work so I can meet with Carter. I'll pick up the kids again from school then come back for you, if you'd like?"

"Are you sure you want to take that much time away from work?"

"I've got the next five hours to get leg work in. Once I have the kids, we'll go back to the hotel for a while so I can work on research and paperwork. A lot of my job is spent sitting at a desk and I can do that from almost anywhere."

Tears unexpectedly spring up in my eyes, "Thank you for everything, I know I would still be in that jail cell if you hadn't shown up. I know you didn't have to bail me out and spend your time chauffeuring the kids around. I will always be grateful to you."

His hand cups my cheek. God, how I have missed being touched.

"You and I are bonded for life. If you need me ten years from now, I will always come for you."

Shit, there goes another pair of panties. At this point I need to start packing extra to just get through the day. He knows exactly what to say to get my juices flowing. With one last smile, he turns back to the road and we enjoy the comfortably quiet ride to work.

Chapter Nineteen

Casey

"Morning, Carter." I hand him a coffee and take a look around the street we're on.

"Hey, Casey, ready to see how screwed we really are?"

I chuckle at his attempt to make light of the uphill situation ahead of us. We had been told the security footage from the club was missing from that night but there is no mention of other camera's in the area. I made the suggestion that we canvas the local businesses around the club and see if anyone has camera's pointed in that direction. If we can find even one that shows Kacee there that night, we can put a huge dent in the prosecution's case.

"Let's start with the closest stores and work our way out."

I grab a pen and notepad, lock up the car and follow Carter to the boutique directly across from the club. I don't see any cameras on the outside but maybe we'll get lucky. The woman behind the counter smiles warmly before going back to her inventory list.

"Good morning, ma'am. My name is Casey Sanders and this is my colleague, Carter Jepsen. We are lawyers working on a case involving the nightclub across the street."

"Oh, I think I heard about that. Some woman attacked a guy in there, right?"

Of course she would only have one side of the story. "I'm afraid we can't go into detail but we were wondering if you have any surveillance cameras that point in that area? We're trying to corroborate statements regarding who was at the club that night."

"As much as I hate that club and wish they would shut it down, I have never bothered with cameras. I'm not open when they are so I mind my business."

"Why do you hate the club?"

"I learned my lesson a few years ago. I mind my business and everything is fine." Her body language and tone make it clear she is done talking to us. I give her my card and ask her to call if she hears anything else about that evening. Carter heaves a weary sigh as he stomps back out on the street.

"I was afraid of this; I think we're going to be hard pressed to find anyone willing to speak out against the Montgomery family."

"You're probably right but I have to try. Come on, let's get this over with."

An hour later, we've struck out with every business on the street. No one has any information to share, and they don't want to get involved either. Frustrated with this whole chicken shit town, I call off the search and head back to our cars.

"Hey, look over there, that store might have cameras."

Glancing across the parking lot, I see a convenience store on the street behind the club. They don't have a view of the front of the club but they are directly across from the parking lot.

"It's worth a try, let's go check it out."

As we enter the store, I notice the sign saying it's open twenty-four hours and there are a few cameras outside. I give the clerk the same spiel as I did the rest of the businesses and hold my breath, praying he has something for us.

"I heard about the incident, can't say I'm surprised with all the crap that goes on in there. Too bad our police department is too scared to do anything about those assholes."

His candor is refreshing and renews my hope. "I noticed some cameras out front, any chance they are pointed toward the parking lot?"

"Yeah, they are, I had to put them in because of that place. I was constantly getting drunks in here in the middle of the night harassing my staff. For the most part, knowing they are being videotaped keeps the creeps away."

"Would you be willing to let us see the footage from that night?"

"Give me a couple minutes and I'll pull it up for you."

He heads through a door behind the counter. I spin excitedly to Carter who is smiling for the first time today. "This is it. I have a good feeling about this one."

"Let's not get our hopes too high yet. We already know it's not going to prove she went into the club."

My cell phone vibrating in my pocket distracts me. Not recognizing the local number, I excuse myself and step outside.

"Hello?"

"Is this Casey Sanders?"

"Yes it is." The woman sounds pleasant, at least I know it's not Dirk with another one of his childish calls.

"I'm calling from Masterson High School, we have Kacee up in the office. There was a bit of an incident today and she's pretty shaken up. She asked us to call you since her mom is out of town."

Kacee lied to them about her mom, that means she doesn't want her knowing what happened. Ten bucks this has something to do with douche bag Dirk. "Yes, I am her father. I can be there in twenty minutes."

"Sounds good, she'll be up here with me till you get here."

Heading back inside, I get to Carter as the shop owner pops back out, letting us know we can come back.

"So that was Kacee's school, apparently there was some kind of incident. I need to go over there and find out what happened. Can you handle this and let me know what you find?"

"Yeah, I got this, go check out what's going on over there. Let me know if it has to do with Dirk and I'll send Officer Freeman over if you need him."

"Sounds good, talk to you soon."

With only a minor amount of speeding, I'm able to get to the school in fifteen minutes. I find Kacee as soon as I enter the office. Her swollen, bloodshot eyes light a fuse inside me. I don't know what happened but I instantly want to hurt whoever made her cry. This new feeling gives me pause; I've never had an aggressive bone in my body. This parenting stuff is sure harder than I thought it would be.

She's out of the chair and crying against my chest before I can introduce myself to the woman behind the desk. I rub her back for a few seconds and let her get the worst of it out. Once she's calmed down a little, I pull her back so I can see her face.

"Are you okay? What happened?" The woman behind the desk clears her throat to get our attention.

"Mr. Sanders, our school resource officer would like to speak with you about the incident."

I nod and look back at Kacee, "Do you want to stay out here or come with me?"

"I'll go with you, it's fine."

I nod and follow the woman down a hallway to a small office at the end that has a huge window overlooking the school's main courtyard. The officer behind the desk stands and shakes hands with me before sitting back down.

"Thanks for coming in. I have to admit, in all my years working here, this is a new one for me. I was patrolling the hallways after lunch when I heard a scream nearby. I found Ms. Celdonio in front of her locker where someone had put quite a few dead rats inside. They weren't just dead; their throats had been cut, too."

Someone is calling her out for ratting them out and I know exactly who is to blame.

"I plan to investigate this thoroughly but I'll be honest with you, I know about the case against the Montgomerys and I'm sure this has something to do with it."

"Can I ask how you are so familiar with the situation?"

"I'm on a bowling league with a few of the guys from the precinct. Steve told me about it and asked me to keep an eye on Kacee for a while."

I'm relieved Officer Freeman had the forethought to get her looked after but since we still don't know who we can trust, I'm hesitant to just accept that he is on our side.

"I was told Dirk is no longer a student here. Any chance he got in the school and did this?"

"We're completely locked down during the day. He would have had to check in at the office and get his license scanned. That's not to say he's not involved, though, his family has friends all over. There are probably fifty kids at this school who would do it if that family asked them to."

"If I were to make a rather large donation to the school, do you think the principal would allow you to have a second officer here for a while? I'd like to pick the person but you can run him through your background checks and all I ask is that he always be assigned to the areas where Kacee is."

"That is a rather unorthodox request but given the circumstances, I might be able to get that approved. Let me talk with the principal and get back to you."

We exchange business cards as the bell rings letting school out. I grab Kacee's backpack and follow her out to the car.

"I'm sorry I freaked out, it was a surprise and the blood was everywhere. I know I overreacted."

"You have nothing to be sorry for and you reacted exactly how most people would in your situation. I have to ask though, why didn't you want them to call your mom?"

Kacee buckles her seat belt and drops her head back against the headrest. "She's in this mess because of me, she doesn't need any more to worry about."

"You know, you're pretty wise for a teenager. While I'm sure she appreciates the gesture, you know we're going to have to tell her, right?"

"Yep, but at least this way she didn't have to miss work again. Maybe we should do it after we give her a few glasses of wine. Soften her up a little, you know?"

"Devious but I like it." My phone rings over the car speakers, interrupting our scheming.

"Hey, Carter, how did it go at the store?"

"I actually got a few things to tell you but first, what happened at the school?"

"It looks like Dirk decided to leave a present in Kacee's locker for her and he thought some mutilated rats were a good idea." I glance at Kacee, who is biting her nails as she listens to our conversation. "I have a plan I'll run by you later. So what did you find out?"

"Well, the good news is the camera's caught Kacee walking from the parking lot around to the front of the club. An hour later, she appears again, running, and you see her disappear between some cars. Thirty minutes later, Brittany shows up and just as she said, she puts Kacee in the car and heads toward the club, then reappears ten minutes later and drives off."

I turn excitedly toward Kacee, who smiles back, even though I'm sure she doesn't understand why I'm so happy. "That is perfect! While we can't prove Kacee was in the club, we have enough to prove reasonable doubt to the other testimonies that she was never there. This is going to be a huge help."

"Well, I wouldn't get too excited yet. I got the call that the venue request was denied. It looks like we're stuck here."

And just like that, it feels like someone punched me right in the gut and knocked all the wind out of my lungs. I pull over and plop my head down on the steering wheel.

"Casey, you still there?"

"Yeah, I'm here. Let me think on all this and I'll call you later to strategize."

"Sounds good, talk to you soon."

I hit the phone button on the car, ending the call. "Excuse me a second."

I jump out of the car and slap the door shut as fifty different emotions running through my body has me pacing back and forth. "Shit...damn...shit...fuck...mother puss bucket." Out of the corner of my eye, I see Kacee staring wide-eyed at me. I probably look like a lunatic. Clearing my throat, I take a deep breath and climb back in.

"Sorry about that, let's go get your brother."

"Is that request getting denied really bad for Mom?"

"I'll be honest with you, it made everything exponentially worse, but I am damn good at what I do and I'm not going to stop until this is over and your mom is acquitted."

"What if I told you I know a way to make Dirk go away for good?"

Chapter Twenty

Casey

"I'm listening."

"I already told you a lot of rumors have been going around. Well, a girl came to me and told me the same thing happened to her. She gave me her cell number and told me to call if I wanted to talk." Her fingers twisting nervously in the braided bracelets on her wrist, I realize how uncomfortable all this is for her and my determination to take down Dirk intensifies a little more. "This got me thinking, what if there are others who have been attacked by him as well? There has always been talk but I've never heard names before. Maybe we could get these girls to come testify against him?"

"So as far as you know, no one has ever reported these crimes?"

"You really don't understand how much power this family has. Everyone knows you can't do anything to stop him."

The look of utter hopelessness on her face hardens something deep inside. If my daughter is going to live in this town, someone needs to take out the trash and that starts with stopping Dirk's reign of terror.

"Let me run all this by Carter then we'll decide what our next move is. The last thing I want to do is make these girls have to relive their stories in a courtroom. We need to go about this delicately, especially since they will likely all be minors and who knows if they've told their parents. I know it's a lot to ask but if she talks to you again, keep in mind her story might have a much worse ending than yours and she may need someone she can talk with honestly."

"Is it wrong that part of me is afraid to talk to her? I don't think I want to hear what she has to say."

The tears welling in her eyes is heartbreaking. This is too much for any woman to deal with, let alone a teenage girl. "You don't have to do anything you don't want to. If you don't want to talk to her then you don't have to."

"If it will help Mom then I want to do this. I heard you outside the car, you put on a good show but I can tell you are worried. Please, let me help."

The determined look in her eyes makes it clear she wants to do this no matter how tough it may be. "How did I get so lucky to have such an amazing daughter?"

"Mom would say good genes." Her laughter breaks the seriousness of the situation.

"That and being raised right. Now let's go get your brother and you guys can go swimming at the hotel while I meet with Carter."

We get in the car line and I text Carter to meet us poolside in twenty. Austin's boundless energy infects the car as soon as he climbs in. It takes very little effort on his part to convince me to order some treats before they swim.

"Kacee, take your brother upstairs and get changed. I'll be down here with Mr. Jepsen catching him up. Snacks will be here when you get back."

As soon as they are on the elevator, I order a few different appetizers and sit down with Carter.

"Here's a copy of the video. Let's hope there are enough anti-Montgomery people left in this city to get a decent jury."

"We may have another angle to go with. It turns out Kacee had a fellow victim reach out to her today and she says there are more. If we can get them to talk, I think we can start a counter suit against Dirk. I think that may be enough pressure to get him to drop his suit."

"I should have thought of that, of course there would be more victims. I don't think you and I should talk to the girls first. What if we get Kacee to quietly spread the word that she is looking for other victims and get them to meet up together? I have a buddy that owns a cafe near the school. He has a private dining room he'll let us use, that way the girls will have a private place to talk. I think we do need an adult in there, though. Do you think Kacee would be okay having Brittany there with her?"

"I'll run it by them but I don't think either would mind. Do you know any crisis counselors that would attend as well in case any of the girls get emotional? I'll pay their fees."

"Let me ask around and get you a name and number."

"Sounds good, I'll text you after they've agreed to the plan. Can you ask your friend to give us the room tomorrow night starting at six o'clock?"

"Shouldn't be a problem at all, see you tomorrow."

Carter leaves as the kids step off the elevator. They fill up on cheese sticks and flat bread pizza before jumping in the pool. I'm still in shock that I'm actually sitting here watching my daughter. The surrealness of the situation takes my breath away. Why am I sitting here watching when I could be living? Isn't that what I've been doing for the last sixteen years?

I tell the kids I'll be right back and after a quick stop in the hotel shop, I buy a bathing suit and get changed. The kids' faces light up when they see me climbing in the pool. I had no idea this was missing from my life till now.

Forty-five minutes later, the alarm on my phone buzzes from the table. "Okay guys, time to get out. Why don't you guys go upstairs and get started on your homework while I run and get your mom. We can order pizza and get through some more of those home movies."

I can see the surprise on Kacee's face. Apparently she did see how upset I got the other night. I have to make sure I control myself better this time.

"Come on, Austin, let's go."

Austin's skinny arms wrap around my waist and squeeze tight. "What's that for?"

"I'm just happy you played with us."

"Swimming with you made me happy, too. Now go with your sister and I'll be back soon."

Once the kids are on the elevator, I change back into my clothes and head to Brittany's office. It has been an eventful day, let's hope she's as excited by the turn of events as I am.

Chapter Twenty-One

Brittany

"Don't think buying me lunch gets you off the hook for not telling me about your baby daddy being in town."

I roll my eyes again for probably the hundredth time today. Sharon has been very clear she isn't happy that I didn't tell her about Casey before now.

"All I'm saying is you never told me about her dad, let alone how gorgeous he is. And you have been dodging my questions about him all day."

"Like I said at lunch, he is here as my lawyer." Of course, this is the last thing I had to say before stepping off the elevator and catching sight of Casey casually leaning against his car with wet hair and looking sexy as hell. I'm not sure who is drooling more, me or Sharon. "Let me get through this trial and I promise I will fill you in on every detail."

"I'll let it go for now but you owe me a bottle of wine and all your secrets cuz damn, that boy is fine."

Casey catches sight of us and electrifies my senses with his gorgeous smile. God, I've missed him.

"Ladies, how was your day?"

"Better now that we've seen you."

I elbow Sharon in the side and shake my head, she is incorrigible.

"I feel the exact same way. If you are ready, the kids are waiting at home."

Sharon's gasp is barely audible but I hear it easy enough and agree with her completely. I spent many nights imagining him saying those words, I never expected to actually hear them. "I'll see you tomorrow, Sharon."

I climb in the car and try to ignore Sharon's smiling face watching as Casey closes my door and runs around the car. She is having entirely way too much fun at my expense. I'm going to remember this next time she goes on a date.

"So the kids and I have already planned out the evening. Once homework is done, we're going to order pizza and watch the rest of the tapes."

"But..."

He holds his hand up to hold me off. "I know I was an idiot last time, but I'm better prepared and promise to handle it better. Now, tell me about your day."

"Nothing really to tell, I sat at my desk, answered calls, went to meetings, pretty mundane. What about you, anything new come up with the case?"

"Well, I have bad news, worse news, good news, and an idea that you may not like."

"Sounds like you've had a busy day, how about you go in that order."

"Bad news, the trial is staying here, our request was denied. Worse news, someone broke into Kacee's locker and left some dead rats inside. Good news, we found video of Kacee heading toward the entrance of the club, coming back out, you showing up and heading to and from the front of the club. Now for the idea..."

"Hang on, take a breath, that was a lot already. I need to process."

His look of dejection makes it clear he was trying to brush over the rat incident.

"First off, I can't believe the school didn't call me. Something like that happens and they don't think it's important enough to tell her parent? I'm going to call her principal tomorrow and give him a piece of my mind."

"Well, technically they did call her parent. Kacee didn't want to upset you so she had them call me instead. But don't worry, I had a good talk with the school resource officer and he's going to try and get approval to let me bring in another guard of my choosing to keep an eye on her."

"I can't believe Dirk did this, why can't he leave her alone? Is she okay?"

"She was upset when I first got there but she's better now. She's actually the reason behind the idea I want to run by you."

"This should be good, let me hear it."

I fill her in on everything Kacee told me and the plans that Carter and I made. The longer I talk, the deeper the creases in her forehead become. I can't tell what emotion they are conveying though.

"So what do you think, will you go with Kacee and help her do this?"

"There are so many parts to this plan that I am not happy with but I see the logic in it. I'm warning you now, though, we aren't going to get pushy with these girls. They've been through enough. If they aren't willing to press charges, I won't get tough with them. I'd rather go to jail than put any of them through any more torture."

"I can respect that; keep in mind you might not hear too much from them right away. It's more important that you tell them what the plan is and what they would need to do. If anyone gets emotional, the counselor will be there to help, but we don't need them to give any details to you. We'll need to make their statements official and if they are minors, we'll need their parents' involvement, too. I know this is going to be hard but I can't stress how important this is for you. We need to take this sick fuck down for all the girls in this town, but we also need him to drop the suit. What do you say, can you do this?"

"Of course I will. These girls need someone to be their voice."

"Okay then, let's get Kacee to start spreading the message around and if we're lucky, we'll get one or two girls to show up."

Chapter Twenty-Two

Casey

Last night went better than expected. We gave Kacee the go ahead to spread the word about the meeting and had Carter get the room for us. With a better sense of how the movies affected me, I was able to keep my emotions under control and enjoy watching the kids grow. It was everything I thought a normal family evening at home would be like. Lord knows I never had one with my parents. The closest I ever came were the nights I hung at Brittany's apartment with her and her mom.

Now sixteen years later, I'm in a restaurant watching from afar as my daughter and her mom prepare to talk to assault victims. This is every parent's nightmare, but the lawyer part of me is hoping for a good turnout. The newly acquired father side of me is praying there aren't many girls forever changed.

"I know it's tough being out here when you want to be in there helping but trust me, they will get more cooperation if there are no men in the room."

I glance at Carter and nod my understanding, it doesn't make it any easier though.

A few minutes later, we watch as two girls come in and head straight for the room. After twenty minutes, we've seen twelve more go in. I can't see most of the room but I have perfect sight of Kacee, Brittany, and the counselor Carter found. Brittany squeezes Kacee's hand before Kacee starts addressing the group. My attention is diverted by a girl that comes in and passes by the room only to turn around and walk by it two more times. I only notice because she keeps breaking my line of sight.

Her stringy hair covers most of her face and she chews her nails as she paces back and forth and glances into the room over and over. I have no doubt she is supposed to be in that room. Not wanting to approach her directly, I text Brittany and fill her in. She leans over, whispering in Kacee's ear before getting up and coming out. The girl darts into the bathroom and Brittany follows right behind her. It feels like forever before they come out and reenter the room.

For the next hour, Carter and I sit in mind numbing silence waiting for the meeting to be over. During that time, I watch as Brittany and the counselor do a lot of talking. Sometimes all three are nodding so I assume some of the girls have opted to talk. I hope that is a good sign some are willing to press charges.

When the first girl leaves the room, we pay our tab and wait anxiously for the girls to join us. After a lot of hugging and a few tears, the last girl leaves and we rush in for an update.

"Well, that was as terrible as I expected it to be." All color is drained from Britt's face; she looks bone-weary and ready to cry.

"I was disheartened to see how many showed up, it reinforces the need we have to stop this guy. Did any of them agree to talk to us?"

"There were fifteen girls here but only thirteen were victims, the other two were friends here supporting each other. Only one said she won't do it, she can't let her family find out. Jeanine gave all the girls her card and offered to talk again if they need it. Hopefully the girls will reach out and get help."

I smile at the counselor, who looks a little worse for wear herself.

"Did you find out how many were minors and tell them we need their parents with them for the interviews?"

"All but two are minors, most of them haven't told their families but seeing how many of them were in this room helped them see they needed to stop him. It was really smart to get them together and let them see they weren't alone."

Kacee's phone buzzes on the table, she smiles before turning back to us. "We asked the girls to spread the word quietly what we are doing. That was one of them saying she messaged her friends. If there are any more of us, they are going to tell them to call you to set up their interviews."

"What about the last girl you brought in, was she the one who refused?"

"I know her from school. Her name is Sarah, she used to be really involved in school. Now that I know she is one of us, I can look back and remember when it happened. She changed overnight, we weren't friends so I didn't really notice or do anything to help her. I feel terrible I didn't see she needed help, how were we all that blind?"

"You can't blame yourself, you are still a kid. You aren't supposed to need to know how to recognize the signs, let alone be expected to do something about it. I hope, though, that you will reach out to her at school. I'm not asking you to be her friend, maybe a smile and a hello will help her."

Brittany's advice is exactly what I would have said. After saying goodbye to Jeanine and Carter, we pick up Austin from his grandmother's and head back to the hotel. The ride is quiet, everyone inside their own heads digesting everything that happened. I can only imagine the things the girls heard in that room, their minds are probably much heavier than mine is.

I wait for Brittany and Austin to walk ahead of us toward the elevators before getting Kacee's attention.

"I wanted to tell you how proud I am of you. We are asking you to do something incredibly difficult. Watching you stand up and get this organized is amazing. Dirk's going to have no idea what hit him."

"I wish I could see his face when he gets served the papers. I haven't decided if he will stomp his foot like he's having a tantrum and run to his parents or if he'll freak out and cry. I've pictured both scenario's in my mind and they both make me happy."

"You definitely can't be there when it happens, but I'll see what I can do to get the scoop on how he handles it."

The elevator arrives and Austin yells for us to hurry up if we want to ride with them. "Actually, Kacee, can you take Austin upstairs? I want to talk to your mom for a bit."

Her knowing smile catches me off guard, "Not a problem at all." She winks and walks on the elevator as she pushes Brittany out. "Go, have some adult time."

She winks at me as the elevator doors slide closed. I think she is trying to play matchmaker.

"What on earth was that all about?"

"I asked her to take Austin up, I thought we could have a drink in the bar?"

Without thinking, my hand slides down her back to the curve at the base of her spine and I lead her to the bar.

"I'll have a Jack and Coke, and the lady will have...?"

"I'll have a Dragon Berry Martini, please."

"That sounds exotic."

"It's really not, Dragon Berry is really a fancy name for Strawberry Rum."

"Well, drink up because you earned it."

I'm mesmerized watching her take a delicate sip. Her eyes close briefly and the softest moan causes desire to flood my body. I'm jealous of that glass getting to touch her soft, luscious lips.

"God, I haven't had one of these in a while. I forgot how good they are. Thank you for this, I really did need it. Being in that room and seeing those girls will haunt me for the rest of my life. You should have seen Kacee, though, I had no idea how strong she was until tonight. We really did make an amazing child." Her hand slides up my chest and stops around the back of my neck. She leans in so we're inches apart and I know she wants me to kiss her but I can't do that to Monica, no matter how much I want to.

"I give full credit to you, it's all in how she was raised. You've done a great job, with both kids." My hand finds my drink and I turn away, pretending to need a drink so I could break away from the temptation. "I was thinking after this is over, maybe I could take the kids home with me so they could meet my parents, maybe a long weekend so they don't miss much school. Would you be okay with that?"

The dejected look on her face means she understood I was pulling away; I hope she understands why I did.

"Have you told your parents about us yet? I'm sure they will be shocked to find out I've turned up after all these years and in the exact kind of trouble they always thought I would be in."

"I thought it would be a fun surprise actually. I know they want Monica and I to start a family as soon as we marry. I'm sure they will be thrilled to have two grandkids to spoil immediately. Who knows, maybe they will be more affectionate with them than they were with me."

The mention of marrying Monica changes the mood instantly. Britt turns back to the bar, finishes her drink quickly and motions for another. For me, saying the words out loud was a wake-up call. I am never going to marry her. It's not fair to either of us and I've dragged it on long enough. As soon as I'm back in town, I'll have to break it off with her. She deserves to marry someone who can love her the way I have always loved Brittany.

She finishes her second drink as we sit quietly and listen to the piano player in the corner. Neither of us is able to think of what to say next after me bringing up my fiancée.

Once her third martini is gone, I realize she should have stopped after two. Her eyes have gone softer and the smile on her face as she sways to the music makes it clear she is relaxed and feeling good. While she's absorbed in the music, I sign the tab to the room and finish the last sip of my drink.

"Ready to go upstairs? I'm sure we'll have a busy day tomorrow so we probably need to get to bed."

"Are you inviting me into your bed?" She gives me a naughty smile then ruins it by almost falling off the bar stool. She's definitely going to need help getting back to the suite.

"Come on, lightweight, let's get you back to your own bed." I grab her upper arm and help her on to the elevator. As soon as the doors close, she pushes me against the wall and kisses me. God, I've waited so long to feel her against me again. I've wanted to kiss her perfect lips from the moment she walked into that room at the jail. Every fiber of my being wants me to give in and take some of the pleasure I've tortured myself over for the last sixteen years. Monica's face flashes in my mind, dousing any momentum I was building. Even if I am calling it off with Monica soon, I am still with her now and I'm not going to cheat on her. I grab Britt's shoulders and push her back from me.

"Why are you stopping? I know you want me and lord knows I need you."

"It's not going to happen like this, now is not the time."

Beautiful, caramel eyes harden instantly and turn away as she stomps off the elevator. Well, as much stomping as she can do as she sways back and forth. My reputation in the courtroom is that I am magic with my words. I can smooth talk a jury and work a witness like no one else can, yet I keep screwing up with Brittany, the one person in the world who I want to talk to most.

She never looks back as she heads straight for her bedroom and closes the door behind her. Maybe I should have invited her to my room. We'd definitely both be a lot more satisfied if I had.

Chapter Twenty-Three

Brittany

The alarm on my phone bores into my consciousness, forcing me out of a hot dream starring Casey. Oh my god, did I really try to get in his bed last night? I knew better than to keep drinking glass after glass but I was wound so tight, I was desperate to relax for a few minutes. How am I going to look him in the eye? Might as well get up and face it like a woman.

With a groan, I sit up on the side of the bed and my mood lightens immediately when I see Austin sleeping on his knees with his butt in the air. I swear that kid is too cute for his own good.

"Wakey, wakey, bud, time to get up. Last day of school for the week then we can sleep in tomorrow."

"Ugh...can't I stay home and play with Casey today?"

"Sorry, he has to work, too. I'm sure you guys will have plenty of time to play this weekend. Now off to the shower, we need to get ready."

Once Austin is showered and dressed, I pour him some cereal and jump into the shower. The water works its magic on me and I feel better almost immediately. Not wasting any time, I wash up and get out, and immediately I hear Casey's booming laugh. He certainly doesn't sound any worse for wear. I didn't watch but something tells me he didn't meet me drink for drink last night. I grab the cheeriest outfit I have and head out, trying to avoid eye contact with Casey. Of course it doesn't last long as he hands me a large hot tea.

"Milk and two sugars, the way you like it." Would he be bringing me a drink if he was mad? I raise hopeful eyes to his and see no trace of anger, maybe I dreamt I asked him to bed?

"Thanks, I definitely need this."

He smiles warmly before turning back to Austin. "Okay, if you guys are ready, the chariot leaves in two minutes."

Austin puts on his backpack and holds Casey's hand out the door. "Mom says we can play this weekend, what do you want to do?"

"Let's see how it goes. I think I'm going to have a bunch of meetings but I'm sure we can carve out some time."

The elevator takes us down quickly; Austin runs ahead to give the valet our ticket. "Do you think you can get your mom to watch him this weekend? I'm going to get the room at the restaurant again. I'm hoping we'll hear from the families and we can set up interviews. Carter is getting a couple of cops that he trusts to be there to fill out the official police reports."

"This is really happening, isn't it? Was it really a week ago that we were both in our own little worlds, oblivious to all of this."

"I know it sucks but I will always be grateful this happened. It led me back to you and I can never wish for anything different."

He holds my car door open on that last little bomb and smiles as I climb in with a shocked smile on my face.

He slides in behind the wheel and pulls out on the road like he didn't just turn my world upside down. I am seriously jealous of Monica, she gets to lay in bed with him every night and be the last person to kiss him before he falls asleep.

"I can probably meet you for lunch if you want. Carter and I are just prepping for the interviews."

"Actually, my mom and grandmother asked if they could meet me."

"That sounds fun, then I'll pick you up this afternoon."

I smile and go back to sipping my tea. I could definitely get used to this.

We pull into the car line, Austin jumps out yelling he loves us and runs inside. A few minutes later, we're in front of my building.

"Thanks for the ride, see you this afternoon." Desperate to get away, I climb out quickly. I can't keep fantasizing about another woman's man, even if he was mine first.

Like yesterday, Sharon is anxiously waiting for me to arrive and give her details about Casey. I blow her off again; how can I talk about him when I don't even know what is going on between us? I really need to see where things go before sharing my deepest secrets with her.

Eager for a mental break, I dive into work and don't even realize lunch time has come. My mother's laughter breaks my concentration. I'm not surprised to find her and my grandmother sitting at Sharon's desk. I have no doubt she is trying to find out what they know without coming right out and asking. The woman is tenacious, I'll give her that.

"Hey, guys, sorry I wasn't downstairs already. I got caught up in work and lost track of time."

"Not a problem, dear." I kiss both on the cheek and stick my tongue out at Sharon as I lead them to the elevator.

It's a short walk to the same diner I ate at with Casey earlier in the week. As soon as we order, the subject I was hoping to avoid is brought up.

"I've waited seventeen years to meet that boy, when are you going to introduce us? I used to love getting those pictures of you guys. Your junior prom picture was breathtaking. He was such a cutie pie and your mama tells me he is one fine piece of meat now."

"Et tu, Mom?"

"What can I say, he has really grown up nicely. I may be old but I'm not dead. I can appreciate a fine ass when I see one."

"And that is exactly why I love you."

My grandmother's frail, wrinkled hand covers mine. "I'm sorry we kept those letters from you. Every year it broke my heart a little more when one would arrive. A part of me wished they would stop arriving so I would know he had moved on. I can't tell you how many times I started a letter back to him to give him some peace, but I knew that would make it worse."

"I was pretty pissed at first but I get it now. You both did what you thought was best and if you hadn't, I wouldn't have Austin. We're all exactly where we are supposed to be right now."

"Well, maybe not exactly where we're supposed to be. I'm pretty sure you aren't supposed to be on trial and I'm supposed to be on a beach somewhere getting lotion rubbed on my back by a twenty-year-old cabana boy."

"I can see you haven't lost your spunk, Grandma."

She cackles hysterically till tears are running down her face. The food comes and we drop the deep conversation and talk about anything and everything but ourselves for an entire forty-five minutes.

As soon as the bill is paid, I see Grandma reach down and pull a box out of her purse. It makes a thud as she puts it on the table then slides it in front of me. I know instantly what's going to be inside and my hands shake at the idea of opening the lid. I desperately want to read every word he has written to me all these years but if I do that now, it will make it that much harder to let him go. I decide right then I won't open them till he is back home in South Carolina and I can grieve for him in peace.

"Thank you for keeping these safe for me."

"You can thank me by letting me meet him tonight at dinner."

"I think he would love to meet you, too."

The walk back to the office feels much different with the box tucked under my arm. How am I going to resist reading them?

Chapter Twenty-Four

Casey

Brittany's smile as she exits the building is electrifying, she still steals my breath away. I've been with her over a week now; you'd think I would be used to her but at least once a day my chest tightens and I go back to the last night I had with her. I remember exactly how she felt in my arms, every look, every smile she gave me. Normally a person wouldn't remember so much detail but if you constantly thought about her being gone for the last sixteen years, you would have those last moments etched in your brain, too.

"You look happy; does that mean you had a good day?"

"Work was fine, lunch with my mom and grandma even better. They want to have dinner with us tonight, Grandma really wants to meet you."

"I'd like to meet her as well. I spent so many years wondering if she was reading the letters or if she even got them. It will be nice to put a face to the person in my memory. Are we inviting them back to the hotel or did you want to eat somewhere else tonight?"

"Let's get the kids from the hotel and eat at an Italian restaurant by our apartment. The food is good and the kids love it there."

"Sounds good to me, I'll never turn down a good bowl of pasta."

"Great, I'll text Mom and get everything set up."

She sends a few texts then puts her phone down. Out of the corner of my eye, I notice she is biting her nail. "Why does it feel like you are stressing over something?"

"Grandma gave me your letters today at lunch."

The punch to my gut is shocking. I knew she would get them eventually but the idea of her having them makes me a little nauseous.

"I haven't opened them yet; I am going to wait till this is over before riding that rollercoaster." I literally sag in relief. "Did you not want her to give them to me?"

"No, I want you to have them. I don't remember everything I've written in them over the years and it is embarrassing to picture you reading them all at once. You have to remember I started sending them when I was sixteen. I'm sure my college years' ones will be entertaining at the least, I had a roommate who was determined to make me loosen up and have fun."

"I'm sure they will be beautiful."

The rest of the ride is filled with awkward silence; my reaction probably threw her off. I didn't expect that shock at such a casual declaration. Now every time I see her I'll be wondering if she's read them yet. Maybe my years of torture aren't over yet.

Desperate to get the mood back, I grasp at anything to talk about. "I meant to tell you, I've been getting calls from the girls wanting to meet with us. We're setting up appointments already, I have a good feeling about this."

"That's awesome, I'm so glad we are going to help them."

"It'll be a long, emotional day. I will let you decide if you think Kacee should be there or not."

"I'll talk to her about it and we'll decide together."

We find the kids watching T.V. when we enter the suite. "Guess where we're going tonight?" Excited faces turn to Brittany expectantly. "We're having dinner with Grandma and Great-Grandma at Donatella's."

Austin cheers and jumps on the couch, "Casey, you are gonna love it. They have a game room and really good ice cream."

"Well then, I can't wait, those are both very important qualifications any good restaurant should have."

"If it's okay, I'd like to take a bath since we have some time till we leave?"

"Sure, I'll entertain the kids," I manage to gasp out as Austin jumps from the couch onto my back and little hands lock around my throat. So this is what parenting is like.

Chapter Twenty-Five

Brittany

I pour a glass of Moscato and sink into the hot water. The bubbles dancing across my skin and popping lightly gives me chills all over. I try to keep my thoughts from straying to the man thirty feet away while I'm laying here naked but it's no use. Before I can chicken out, I turn the music on my cell phone and get lost in my own pleasure as quietly as I can.

Sated and slightly embarrassed by what I did, I climb out and dry off. The knock at the door surprises me.

"Yes?"

"Hey, I laid out some clothes for you."

"Um...thanks?"

I hear the bedroom door shut and peek into the room. No one is around but there is a red dress I bought three years ago on a whim lying on the bed next to a pair of shoes that I've only worn once. Both items were splurges that I never got any use of as a single mom with no social life. On the dress is a note: "Don't even think about coming out of this room wearing something different. Show him what he's missing out on." I can't believe Kacee packed these, she obviously has ulterior motives.

She's right, though, why not show that I still have the goods? Excitement bubbles in my stomach as I slip on the dress and do my hair and makeup. As I'm buckling my shoes, Kacee slips into the room.

"Oh my god, Mom, you look hot! Dad's not going to know what hit him."

As good as her comments make me feel, I need to make sure she doesn't get overly optimistic. "Sweetie, you know he's going home, right? He has a fiancée and a career waiting for him."

"I'll believe it when he's actually gone." With a wink she slinks back out the door and I'm left with butterflies as I step out to follow her.

With a quick glance around the room, I see the guys on the couch. I try to avoid attention by grabbing my purse and heading straight for the door, yelling over my shoulder, "I'm ready when you are, let's go."

"Mommy, you look so pretty." I love my children but do they have to make it sound like I'm a complete frump the rest of the time?

"Thanks, sweetie, now let's go get dinner."

My hand reaches the doorknob as Casey catches up and grabs my arm. At first his mouth opens and closes a few times like a fish till he finally manages to blink and regain function. "My god, you take my breath away." The fire in his eyes makes it clear what he thinks. For a few seconds neither of us move, so many unspoken emotions shooting between us. The tension is so palpable even Austin would have picked up on it had Kacee not led him to the elevator.

"Thanks, it's feels good to play dress up once in a while."

"You deserve to feel like this all the time."

"Come on, guys." Austin breaks the spell, yelling down the hall while he holds the elevator doors open. I hear Casey clear his throat and take a deep breath. I think tonight is going to be a lot more fun than I expected.

The ride to the restaurant is definitely odd. Austin entertains us with stories from the playground while I see Casey glance over at me constantly. It's almost like he's trying to memorize every detail. I know exactly how he feels, the kids and I will remember these days as a pseudo-family for the rest of our lives.

As a last minute stroke of genius, I grab my phone and text Mom. "Preparing you guys now, Kacee played dress up with me. Please don't make a big deal, I'm nervous enough."

"LOL, I'll be good but I can't make any promises for your grandmother ;)"

Great, let's hope she's so distracted by meeting Casey that she won't notice me. We pull into a parking spot and see them standing by the door waving at us. Let the games begin.

Chapter Twenty-Six

Casey

I don't think I've taken a breath since Brittany walked out of that bedroom. Holy shit, she looks amazing. How am I going to keep my hands off her? Part of me wishes I had already broken up with Monica and that the kids were spending the night at Grandma's. It's going to take every ounce of willpower I have not to ogle her all night. Am I really expected to make a good impression with her grandmother when the blood has left the head on my shoulders?

Spotting Maria and the infamous Grandma Louise, I finally see where Brittany got her looks from. Her auburn hair and caramel eyes were always a stark contrast to her mother's blonde hair and green eyes. I never understood how they could be related. Grandma Louise looks like a much older version of Britt.

"Are you ready for this?"

I look over to Britt's mischievous smile; I have a feeling Louise is a saucy lady. "Yep, let's do this."

I stand back and let everyone take turns hugging. Before I can introduce myself, Louise reaches up and cups my face. "So this is your soul mate, Brittany? You're quite the looker, aren't you?"

"Grandma, oh my god." I hear the kids chuckling behind me while Britt looks on in horror.

"Um, thank you."

"Can we go inside and sit down, please?" Britt attempts to get everyone inside while Louise locks arms with me, effectively making sure I escort her in.

"I gotta tell you, I'm actually a little sad you are here. Even though I never opened those letters, I always got joy from seeing them arrive. I'm a romantic at heart so seeing your loyalty and dedication never waning in all these years touched me."

"I'm impressed you managed to resist not opening them. I don't think I'd have had that kind of willpower."

"It was enough for me knowing you were still thinking about her."

Once Louise is seated at the table, I take my seat next to Brittany and take a breath to soak in the moment. Every once in a while it hits me out of nowhere, this is what I could have had if she hadn't left. A family dinner in a restaurant where the employees stop by to say hi because we are regulars. I'm pulled from my thoughts when the waiter takes everyone's drink order. Bread and an oil-based dip are set in the center, and everyone digs in. With her first bite, Brittany let's out one of those sexy little moans of hers. Sweet Jesus, how am I going to make it through the night? Her dress is lower than anything she's worn so far, her breasts have filled out with age and its torture seeing them out of the corner of my eye. I'm not normally such a lecher but this is Brittany, the woman I've fantasized about for half my life.

Throughout the meal, Louise bombards me with questions. It feels like I'm being interrogated. Brittany gives Austin money for the game room when the case comes up. We fill them in on the plan and they are just as shocked at the number of girls who have come forward.

As dessert is delivered, Austin runs up and hands me a folded piece of paper. Curious, I open it, and dread fills my body.

All this trouble and I didn't even get the girl.
Maybe she won't be so lucky next time.

"Austin, who gave you this? Where did you get it from?"

The tone of my voice scares him and he shrinks into his seat.

"Casey, what is it? What's wrong?"

I hand Brittany the note before going over and kneeling next to Austin's chair. "I'm sorry, buddy, I didn't mean to scare you. I really need you to tell me where you got that paper."

"A guy came in and played the basketball toss game, then he came over to me and asked if I was with you and I said yes. He asked me to give you that. Did I do something wrong?"

"No, you didn't, but he's not a very nice man and if you see him again, I want you to come get one of us right away, okay?"

He nods meekly. I hand him the rest of my cheesecake and sit back down.

"I can't believe that little prick came in here. He's obviously following us or someone here called him."

"These are good people we've known for years, it's more likely he followed us. How are we going to keep the kids safe? I don't want them to feel like prisoners because of him."

"Let's finish our evening and talk about it later." Kacee has been getting more and more anxious to know what is happening. I don't want to scare her, better to change the subject for now. Plus, if Dirk is watching, it should piss him off to see us acting indifferent.

"I don't know about you guys but this is the first weekend off I've had in a long time. Why not order another bottle of wine?" I signal the waiter and relax into my chair. You can suck it, Dirk Montgomery.

Chapter Twenty-Seven

Brittany

Every movement I've made has been done precisely and intentionally. If I'm going to get gussied up, I might as well take advantage of it. As subtly as possible, I show off my cleavage. It feels good to have someone to show off to. It's been way too long since someone has appreciated me or my assets.

It was a perfect night until that note showed up. Of course Dirk would even have to taint this place. That last bottle of wine was a symbol of stubbornness and a middle finger to him. He will not control us.

We finally wind down the night and say goodbye to Grandma and Mom with the promise that Casey will see her again soon. I think she's in love.

At the hotel, the kids put on a movie in the living room and I join Casey on his balcony. The stars shining brightly always make me feel peaceful.

Casey gets my attention with a heavy sigh. "I was thinking I would hire some private security guys to come in and watch the kids discreetly. They probably can't get in the school but I think we have that taken care of, at least for Kacee. I don't think Austin will have a problem at his school. What do you think?"

"It's probably not a bad idea since he's about to be arrested and put on his own trial. Plus, you are getting the restraining order for Kacee."

"Sure, I'll work with Carter to get it taken care of." He grabs my hand and squeezes, "You looked beautiful tonight, and I'm really glad I got to meet Louise. She is everything I thought she would be and more."

"If you're not careful, she may try to steal you for herself."

"I believe you are right." Once the laughter dies down, I realize his hand is still on mine. The warmth radiating from his skin to mine sends chills up my arm. His thumb strokes the top of my hand lightly, I don't even think he knows he is doing it. Not wanting the spell to be broken, I close my eyes and focus on his touch.

"Relax, I'm taking you inside."

His words barely register as I feel myself being lifted out of the chair into his arms. "What's going on?"

"You fell asleep. I put the kids to bed already, now it's your turn."

The mixture of cologne and his own scent flood my senses. Curling against him, I cuddle in and take advantage of his pampering, something I haven't experienced in many years.

He lays me gently on the bed and pulls the covers up. I hear my own sigh when his lips touch my forehead as he says good night. I curl into the pillow and fall asleep peacefully.

Chapter Twenty-Eight

Casey

"Time to get up, we have to meet Carter in an hour." Hopefully they hear me so I don't have to barge in. I knock again, waiting for some noises.

"We're up, give us a few minutes and we'll be ready."

Twenty minutes later, everyone emerges fresh-faced and ready to go.

"We're going to drop Austin off to your mom's then grab breakfast at the restaurant before everyone starts showing up. Maria is going to take Austin out for a big brunch."

"Sounds good, let's go."

We get to Maria's quickly and Austin grudgingly agrees to go after I promise to go swimming with him later. As we get closer and closer to the restaurant, I see Kacee getting more anxious. She's biting her nail and I can hear the whisper of her jeans against the leather indicating she is shaking her leg up and down.

"Are you okay?"

Her eyes meet mine in the mirror and the panic is clear. "Yeah, I'm fine, just nervous about meeting all the girls again with their parents and knowing what they are about to do. It's pretty heavy for a Saturday morning."

"Yes, it is but don't worry, we're all going to do this together."

We pull into the lot as Carter walks inside. We meet him at a large table next to the private room and order breakfast. While we eat, I catch him up on the note and getting a restraining order.

As we're finishing up, Officer Freeman and another officer come in and sit down.

Carter shoves his plate away and pulls out a notebook. "Thanks for agreeing to come, gentlemen. We're going to have to move fast to try and keep this quiet. I've done all the pre-work, as soon as their statements are taken we'll get the arrest warrant out and get this douche behind bars."

"Do I get to know who the perp is now?" The officer I don't know asks as he looks between Officer Freeman and Carter. They exchange glances and Carter nods.

"You are going to take statements from almost a dozen females who will say they were assaulted by Dirk Montgomery." I watch the officer's eyes bulge slightly before he clears his throat and regains composure. "Officer Freeman is vouching for you that we can trust you to keep this confidential and be careful about anyone else in the precinct asking questions they shouldn't be. So, are you up for this?"

"I went to school with Dirk's older brother. That kid made my life hell and got away with it. I'll be happy to take down anyone I can in that family."

"All right then, you guys will be in the room with me. As each family arrives, Casey is going to be out here. He'll bring them in as they are ready. Let's get set up, the first family should arrive in a few minutes."

A few minutes later, one of the girls from the other night walks in with her mother. Kacee waves them over and they sit down.

"This is Emily, she's in school with me."

She smiles and shakes hands with each of us. I'm relieved she seems to be handling this really well. I think I was expecting them to come in crying and scared.

"This is my mom, Theresa."

"I want to thank you all for doing this. Emily told me about what happened, the cop who came to the house didn't believe us and told us to drop it if we knew what was good for us." She smiles at Emily and squeezes her hand, "We thought it was over and he was going to get away with this."

"I have no doubt we can put him away, but it's going to be uncomfortable and you are going to have to tell your story a few times. If you are ready, we have officers in the next room ready to take your statement."

"I've been ready to do this for over a year. I'm pissed and I want this over."

I smile at Kacee and Brittany and take the girls into the room. Now comes the hard part, hearing their stories.

Chapter Twenty-Nine

Brittany

The first three families that came in were in control and eager for justice. I should have known it was too good to be true to expect all of the families to be that easy. Sarah, the timid girl that I had to convince to come in to the meeting, walks in with an angry looking man. She looks as miserable as she did the other night. Kacee waves and gives her a genuine smile. The man pulls the chair out and sits roughly.

"My niece tells me we have to come talk to the cops but she won't tell me why. None of you look like cops so someone better explain what's going on."

My jaw falls open, how could it not? This poor girl hasn't told him what happened to her and she's obviously afraid to. I squeeze Kacee's hand, who thankfully gets the message.

"Sarah, can you go to the bathroom with me? Mom always wants me to go in pairs."

As soon as the girls are out of earshot, I nod to Casey to break the news.

"My name is Casey Sanders, I'm a lawyer here working on a case. This is a sensitive issue and Sarah is a minor. Can you tell me why you are here instead of her parents?"

His eyes close while he takes a deep breath. "Her parents were killed when she was three, I'm her legal guardian."

"I'm sorry to hear that, she has already obviously been through a lot. During our investigation, it was discovered that a number of girls were assaulted by Dirk Montgomery. Your niece came to us saying she was one of those victims."

A horrified look crosses his face; I know that look well. It's the same one I had when I first got Kacee's voicemails that night.

"I knew something happened to her. She changed suddenly but she wouldn't open up to me. I tried having my girlfriend talk to her but it was a no go, she wouldn't talk. I can't believe she didn't tell me. She's been so different the last year, I assumed I was going to see the cops today because she got busted doing something."

"I'm going to take you and Sarah in the next room. She will give her statement to two police officers. There is another lawyer inside named Carter Jepsen who is working this case with me. As soon as we have the girls' statements, we're going to secure an arrest warrant and get him locked up."

"You better put him away or I might have to do something to him next time I see him."

"You are all that Sarah has and she is bound to struggle with retelling her story so I hope you can keep your calm, let us do our job and you focus on taking care of your niece."

He nods and drops his head, the sign of broken man. I'm sure he's feeling like a failure; I sure have many times since that night.

The girls come back and Sarah is looking nervously at her uncle. At first I'm afraid he's not going to make eye contact, but thankfully after a second, he stands up and wraps her in a bear hug. Her entire body tenses before collapsing into it and sobbing.

Casey ushers them into the room so they can have more privacy. My whole body relaxes; she is going to get the help she needs now to move on.

Six hours later, we've met seven more families, and two of them were girls who hadn't been at the original meeting. The number of victims continue to climb and with each girl who sits at our table, another level of hatred builds. Justice better be on our side, because this town deserves a little retribution.

"Okay, ladies, we're done for the night. We have more interviews tomorrow starting around eleven a.m." Casey looks ragged around the edges, much like the rest of us. He was in the room, though, I know he heard every detail so he is probably a lot worse off than Kacee and me.

"Thank you all for putting in such a long day. I hope you realize how important this was for all of us." Both officer's shake our hands with the promise they will be back tomorrow.

"We better go get Austin; he's probably driving my mother up the wall. If you are too tired to swim, I can get you out of it."

"More than anything I think hanging with you guys in the pool is exactly what we all need."

"Carter, you are welcome to join us if you'd like."

"You don't want to see this old body in a bathing suit. Besides, I'm pretty tired. I'll see you guys in the morning."

With pizza in hand for Austin, we head out for a few hours of innocent fun to distract us from the evil we've been dealing with.

Chapter Thirty

Casey

Sunday was as bad as Saturday. I sit at that table in our makeshift office at the station trying to concentrate and take notes but also trying to keep my emotions in check. I'm going to make this family pay; they are going to pay for every girl their son bothered. You don't get looked at for District Attorney in your early thirties unless you are good at what you do. I am damn good and now I'm pissed, too, and I've set my resolve to watching their world crumble around them.

"We got it. Freeman has the warrant and they are heading to the house now to arrest him. Want to go watch from a distance?" Carter's look of absolute excitement is contagious.

"Absolutely, plus I promised Kacee I would tell her how he reacts."

"Then let's go." He spins on his heel and leaves the precinct faster than I've seen him move since I met him.

Officer Douglas has the warrant in hand as he grimly climbs in his cruiser. I know what he heard over the last two days has changed him forever like the rest of us. He thought he hated the Montgomery family before but like me, he has a new sense of determination to take them down. Maybe this will be the beginning this town needs to oust that family and take back control.

Thirty minutes later, we pull up in front of a huge house set on a couple of acres. The cruiser pulls right up to the door but I park my car on the street out front. We watch as the officers ring the doorbell and wait for it to be opened.

"I feel like we should have brought popcorn. I can't wait to see this little shit's face."

An older Hispanic woman opens the door, talks for a minute then closes the door. A minute later, Dirk is at the door with a man that looks exactly like he does, just older. The papers are handed over and as expected, we can see Dirk's face contort with rage, then he leans toward Freeman looking like he's about to swing when his dad pulls him back. They exchange words before Dirk finally steps out and lets them handcuff him. I snap a picture on my cell phone and wait while the cruiser slowly drives past us. I roll down my window and wave as Dirk starts screaming when he sees us. Sometimes I love my job.

As expected, a lawyer is already at the station when we get there, and Dirk's father isn't far behind. He speaks to their lawyer for a few minutes, glancing at Carter and me repeatedly. I take my first sip of coffee when Mr. Montgomery stalks over to us.

"You are looking pretty smug. Do you really think he's going to stay in here? You're new around here so I suppose you don't know how things work but you, Mr. Jepsen, know exactly what you've gotten yourself into."

"You don't have to be in this town long to know there is a degenerate family bullying everyone around them. I'm looking forward to taking your son down." I toss the coffee in the garbage next to the desk and walk away. I hear expletives behind me. As hoped, my coffee had splashed on his perfectly pressed pants.

"Holy shit, Casey, I knew the moment I met you, you were tough but that was out right insane. You just drew a target on your back."

"Are you sure you want to move to Florida after this case? I have a feeling things are going to get very interesting around here."

"You are one crazy son of a bitch. Now let's go see if we can watch them taking his mug shot and prints. Freeman and Douglas have to be loving this."

"Kacee and Brittany would probably love a couple more pictures."

As discreetly as possible, I snap photos when I can, trying to document every level of humiliation he goes through. I know this isn't professional but he did go after my daughter.

Freeman stops by our little conference room and lets us know the lawyer has a tight rein on Dirk and he isn't letting him say anything. It doesn't matter, though; we have enough evidence to ensure he is put behind bars for a very long time.

They move Dirk to holding to wait for his arraignment, and it's no surprise they got a judge to hear his case immediately. Carter and I grab lunch then head for the courthouse. I have tried hundreds of cases in my career and never have I felt more determined and battle ready as I do now.

Kacee and Brittany smile and wave from the front row in the courtroom. I knew when I called them to give them the good news they would be excited, but I didn't expect them to be here. I really shouldn't be surprised, though, they are both very strong-willed women and I wouldn't want it any other way.

"Are you sure you guys want him to see you? He's already got it out for you, it will only make it worse if he thinks you orchestrated this."

"I appreciate your concern but I want to look him in the eye when he enters the room. I want him to know exactly who is doing this."

"You ladies are tough. I don't know why Dirk even thought of messing with you two."

Dirk's case number is called. Carter and I take our places and watch smugly as he is brought in. At first he seems calmer, more so than he has all day. My guess is his daddy and lawyer told him everything was taken care of. The look on his face when he sees Brittany and Kacee is a moment I want etched in my memory forever. His face turns from shock to hatred in seconds. It's amazing how ugly that can make a person look. His lawyer whispers in his ear when he gets to the table and his face changes drastically to a look of innocent fear. What a great actor he is.

The charges are read, the not guilty plea entered. His lawyer asks for him to be released into his parents' custody until the trial.

Carter jumps to his feet immediately, "Your Honor, we have seventeen women who wouldn't be able to sleep tonight if you let him free. This isn't a case of burglary, your Honor. He physically and emotionally assaulted every one of these women and does not deserve to be let out. Not to mention with his family's money and connections, he is a flight risk."

I'm impressed by his speech; I don't think I could have done better myself. Dirk's lawyer counters that he will surrender his passport in an act of good faith. They can't possibly think that will work.

"I will release Mr. Montgomery; bail is set at five million dollars. You must not go anywhere besides home and work; you will be fitted with an ankle monitor until the time of your trial. Also, you are not to go within 100 yards of any of the women named in this suit."

Utter shock and bewilderment course through my body. Five million is nothing for this family. I guess we know which side this judge favors.

Dirk's father seems thrilled. He, on the other hand, is shooting daggers at Brittany. Spoiled little brat thought he was going to get out of this easily like he has everything else in life. His mood gives me some solace.

"Come on, Casey, all things considered I think we got the best we were going to get. How about we all go out for a celebratory dinner?"

"Let me see how they are feeling, one minute."

With an apology on my lips, I'm stopped by Brittany's arms wrapping around me. "Thank you."

"How can you thank me? He's not going to jail."

"Not yet he isn't, but I think he knows we're serious and his parents are going to keep him on a tight leash if they have any expectation of winning the case."

"You are still the optimist I remember you being. What about you, Kacee, are you and the girls going to be okay knowing he's out?"

"You did great, Dad. Besides, I'm with you guys, I know I have nothing to worry about. I'll tell the other girls to stay in for the night if they can. I think everyone's going to be a lot more cautious for a while."

"So how about it, are we celebrating?"

Carter joins our circle and accepts a hug from Brittany.

"Carter wants to get dinner, okay with you guys?"

"Sure, I'll have Mom and Austin meet us. Where should I tell them we're going?"

"How about that seafood place over on Sixth Street?"

"You mean the one directly across from the restaurant the Montgomery's own and Dirk works at?" Brittany's shocked face and Carter's gleeful expression make it clear she thinks his plan is insane.

"Now who's the crazy son of a bitch?" Carter continues to surprise me.

"I'm going to pick up my wife, we'll meet you there soon."

Chapter Thirty-One

Brittany

I understand why they would want to go to this restaurant but I'm not thrilled with the decision. It's one thing to show fearlessness and quite another to poke the bear.

There is a short line at the valet stand and while we wait our turn, I can't help but inspect the restaurant across the street. At a glance I don't see Dirk or anyone from his family inside; maybe we'll get lucky and there won't be any drama.

Carter pulls up behind us and we're introduced to his wife before we all go inside. I notice I'm not the only person keeping a watchful eye across the street. In the few minutes we're on the sidewalk, I see both Casey and Carter look over a handful of times.

"Mom is already inside with a table, should we join her?"

The planets must be aligned; we're given the table directly in front of the window. Not only can we see their restaurant perfectly, but they will be able to see us easily if they happen to look over.

Carter waves the waiter over. "How about we skip the wine and go right to champagne?"

"Sounds good to me, we need to toast the best legal team in Utah." Mom wanted to come to the hearing but I wouldn't let her. I want her and Austin away from this as much as possible. I texted her the outcome and she was thrilled, apparently she wasn't the only one who thought he was going to walk out of there free and clear.

"I'm starving, let's order, too."

Four courses and two bottles of champagne later, we decide to call it a night. I think everyone is going to crash after the weekend we've had.

"Mom, give me your valet ticket. Will you keep the kids in here while we get the cars? I don't want them outside for long."

"Sure, sweetie, I'll entertain them at the lobster tank."

We follow the Jepsen's to the valet stand. Three other couples are already in line, so we're forced to wait. I appear to be the only one worried about this.

"Casey, why don't you come to my office tomorrow and we'll get some more work in?"

"Geez, honey, you guys worked all weekend, can't you take a day off?" Carter strokes his wife's cheek lovingly.

"How about I promise to work a half day? I don't want to lose any momentum on either case."

The valet walks by and collects our tickets, we're almost out of here. I can't wait to get in the car and get home. I haven't relaxed in hours.

"Check it out, we've got fans."

Over Casey's shoulder, I see two men staring at us and talking to each other animatedly. Finally, one goes inside and to my dread I see Dirk step out with him in tow. Of course he had to work tonight. Carter raises his hand and waves across the street.

"You son of a b…" In his rage, Dirk takes off at a run toward us. He never saw the bus coming and it didn't even have time to hit the brakes.

Screams reverberate up and down the street. In shock, I spin into Casey's arms and close my eyes. It doesn't help, the image of Dirk getting hit is seared in my brain.

"I can't believe he did that."

"I guess he was dying to talk to us."

My jaw drops as I stare at Carter, shocked by his words. His wife slaps him on the shoulder, apparently she didn't like his pun either.

"Too soon? Look, I'm sorry it happened but come on, it's not like he was a good guy lost too soon."

"I'm going to go inside; I don't want the kids coming out." Hands shaking, I go inside and try to compose myself. Tears are rolling down my face, not for Dirk, per say, I think it's more a reaction to the situation and for his mother, too. No matter what he's done, he is still her boy.

"What happened out there? People are saying someone got hit."

"Yeah, it's not pretty. Your car is here, can you take the kids to the hotel and get them to bed? We'll probably be here a while."

"Are you sure you are okay? You are so pale."

"I'm fine, I'll explain later."

Enough police and ambulances arrive to block the kids from seeing anything. I kiss them goodnight and tell them we'll be home later.

Long after the car is gone, I continue staring down the street, trying to process what happened.

"Did you tell them?" Casey's hands land on my shoulders and squeeze. In need of his warmth, I lean against his chest and take a deep breath.

"No, let them sleep tonight."

"If you are ready, we're giving witness statements. The sooner we do this, the sooner we can go home."

"Yeah, I want to be gone before his parents get here."

The pro to now having friends on the police force and your party being respected lawyers, we are able to give our statements first and they let us go.

"This is going to change everything; we definitely need to strategize first thing in the morning."

Part of me is surprised by Carter's ability to focus on the case at hand and think about what this accident means for us. These thoughts are furthest from my mind.

The ride back to the hotel is quiet; shock will do that. At the hotel, Casey fills Mom in on what happened and I can tell her tears are of relief. I don't blame her and I don't think that makes her a bad person either.

"I think I'm going to call in tomorrow and keep the kids home. I know Casey has a lot to do so if you want to come hang out with us, we will be here all day."

"Sounds good, sweetie, see you tomorrow."

Emotionally drained, I collapse on the couch as soon as she's out the door. Casey sits next to me and wraps his arm around my shoulders.

"I admit when I woke up this morning, this is not how I pictured this day would end."

I laugh at his understatement of the year. "You and me both."

Tilting my head back, I stare into his beautiful blue eyes, "Thank you for being so amazing today."

The pull between us is almost unbearable. I can see the pain and longing in his eyes, they likely mirror mine. We move at the same time, our lips touch and I'm transported back to our last night together. Every feeling I had for him pours out of me and into that kiss. Desperation eats at both of us and I eagerly straddle his hips when he turns me toward him. Breathless minutes go by, my heart beating out of my chest. My god, I've missed this man.

"Take me to bed," I whisper shyly against his neck.

Without a word, he stands up with me still straddling him. I wrap my legs around his hips and kiss him all the way to his bed. You would think sixteen years of yearning would make us explosive, instead there is a fragile melding of hearts and bodies. My last thought as he lays on top of me is how much I love him.

Chapter Thirty-Two

Casey

I wake up with Brittany in my arms. For a fleeting moment I thought it was another dream. I could smell her, feel her, listen to her breathing deeply in sleep. I laid there for a long time, trying to absorb every detail. As the sun starts peeking through the blinds, I wake her with a kiss.

"Sorry to wake you, I thought you might want to be on the couch before the kids get up."

"Can we have five more minutes before we break the spell and let the day start?"

Words aren't needed; I wrap my arms around her and hold tight. Our bodies have changed over the years but she still feels perfect against me.

Her nails lightly stroking up and down my back threaten to put me back to sleep. If we don't break the spell, as she says, we'll be discovered because I won't be letting her out of my bed.

"When I leave, do you want me to order room service?"

"No, I think we'll eat by the pool and spend most of the day down there. We could use a few hours of mindless fun."

"I'll be jealous the whole time I'm gone."

"Then you better hurry home and join us."

The idea of rushing home to her after a day at work is exactly what I want to be doing for the rest of my life. Before we can worry about that, we have to keep her from going to jail.

"I'm guessing you don't want to put the same clothes on. I have a couple of t-shirts in the drawer that I haven't worn yet, maybe the kids won't notice?"

"Kacee will definitely notice, she will probably be thrilled though. Austin is thankfully still innocent and wouldn't put a thought to it."

Picturing our daughter knowing we had sex freaks me out a little, but then again what part of any of that sentence doesn't? The part where I say our daughter or the part where we had sex?

"Help yourself to a shirt, I'm going to jump in the shower."

"I'd love to join you but we better not risk it."

The picture she put in my head forces out every other thought. "I suggest you run out of here quickly if you don't want me to lock you in for a while."

She giggles and lunges for the dresser. Smart idea.

Lucky for me, I'm dressed and ready to go before the kids have woken up. It allows me to give Brittany a kiss goodbye. Life has become surreal and I don't want it to end.

I open the door to leave and see the daily newspaper on the ground. Most mornings I toss it on the counter for later but I can't this time. A large picture of Dirk is splashed across the front page. Someone must have stayed up all night to get this story printed. I stuff the newspaper in my bag and head to Carter's office. I'll read the article when I get there, I'm curious to see what kind of spin the writer put on the story.

After a quick pit stop for donuts and coffee, I get to the office as Carter is pulling up. He takes the coffees from me so I can grab everything else.

With his free hand, he holds up the newspaper tucked under his arm. "Did you see the paper yet this morning?"

"I brought it with me so I could read it. Have you read it?"

"Not yet, let's get settled in and see what it says."

I follow him into the small office building, it is dated but functional and clean. I grab a donut and start the article. Three pages are dedicated to this guy. They talk about both trials and the accident itself. I'm surprised to read a very impartial view of everything. I guess the Montgomery's haven't gotten to them yet.

"All things considered, it's a pretty decent article."

I nod my head at Carter's opinion. As he reaches for a second donut, his desk phone rings.

"This is Carter Jepsen, how may I help you?"

I see him look up at me, surprised. He mumbles a couple of okays and yeses before finally hanging up. That one-sided conversation gave me no indication as to what that was all about.

"Well I'll be damned, that was the Montgomery's lawyer. He wants to know if we will bring Brittany here this afternoon. Mrs. Montgomery and her lawyer would like to meet with us."

Utter confusion crosses my face, "What could she possibly want to talk about? I'm surprised she is still functioning."

"I've watched her grow up, she's a tough lady. She was a sweet kid till Julius Montgomery got his hands on her. You could actually see her change over the years and not exactly for the better. I agreed to have Brittany here at three p.m. If she doesn't want to, I'll call back and cancel."

"I'll call Brit and let her know, I'm sure she'll agree."

I grab my coffee and head outside. I click the picture of Brittany's smiling face and wait for her to pick up.

"You miss me this soon?"

"You sound even sexier than you did last night. You have a great phone voice." Her laughter is music to my ears.

"Maybe if you are good, I'll show you how sexy I can be."

"I am definitely going to take you up on that offer but first, I have some business to discuss."

"Uh-oh, that doesn't sound good." She sighed.

"I can't really say if it's good or bad but Mrs. Montgomery and her lawyer would like to meet with you at three here at Carter's. Are you good with that?"

"What do you think she wants?"

"I can't say for sure. I'll see if Officer Freeman is available to hang nearby in case there is an incident but Carter says she isn't bad so I think we'll be okay. Plus, you have me there to protect you."

"As sexy as that sounds, I think I can take her if necessary." We both laugh, imagining Brittany grabbing Mrs. Montgomery in a headlock is quite the picture.

"I'm not happy about this but I'll meet with her. Mom is already here; I'll ask her to watch the kids."

"Sounds good, oh and don't have too much fun there without me."

"I promise to keep our fun level to a minimum. See you in a few hours."

Chapter Thirty-Three

Brittany

Driving to Carter's office, I can't help biting my nails. I have no idea what Dirk's mom could want, why she's meeting without her husband, and if she is even in her right mind given she lost her son last night.

I managed to still have fun today, I tried to put it out of mind as much as possible and just enjoy being with my family. After being with Casey every day for the last couple of weeks, it is actually odd to be doing something without him. I miss him and I can tell the kids feel his absence as well. When he leaves, we're all going to be devastated.

I pull into Carter's and put aside my melancholy thoughts. I find the boys huddled over their note pads throwing ideas out at each other. It's kind of cute to see them so absorbed they don't even realize I've walked in.

"You two look like you are hard at work."

"Holy cow, is it time already? Man, this day flew by." Carter leans back and rubs his eyes.

My stomach does a little flip as Casey walks toward me and kisses me on the cheek. "How was your day?"

"It was terrible, we did nothing fun and pined for you all day."

"I didn't say you couldn't have any fun, I said keep it to a minimum."

"Darn, I guess I missed that part." I wink and head toward the conference table, leaving him in my wake. A girl doesn't want to appear too eager.

"Are you ready for this?" Carter's seemingly innocent question makes me take a deep breath.

"Of course I am ready to meet with the mother of my daughter's tormentor who we just had arrested and now he's dead. This should be a lovely tea party." He stares at me, eyebrows half way up his forehead. I don't think he knows how to take that. "I mean, yep, ready as I'll ever be."

As we settle in, the door opens. Our guests walk in, Mrs. Montgomery has large sunglasses on and isn't smiling. Her lawyer is a silver-haired man in his fifties and unlike Carter, he is dressed in a fancy suit and exudes power. He holds the chair out for his client as she takes her glasses off and stares straight at me. Her eyes are red and swollen. Large bags are drooping below her eyes; this is a broken woman.

"Mrs. Montgomery, we are sorry for your loss." Her eyes flash to Casey and she gives him a small nod before returning her attention to me.

"I know you think my son was a monster, and until a few days ago I would have vehemently denied that. I can see now I was blind to his true character. There are people in my family who can be, let's just say, bad influences." She pauses to clear her throat; I can hear her struggling to keep her emotions in check. "Dirk was a good boy. I had hoped I could keep him from following in his father and brothers' footsteps. When he turned fourteen, I figured out that I couldn't save him either but I promise you, I had no idea how bad he had gotten."

A single tear rolls down her cheek. She pulls a tissue from her purse and wipes it away while staring off to the side. I have no idea how to respond so I keep quiet. We all do.

"When I found out about your case, I begged him to tell me the truth and he swore up and down that he hadn't touched your daughter. I'm his mother, what could I do but believe him? When the police showed up to arrest him, my husband was completely unfazed but I was shocked. I couldn't believe the allegations. There had never been any whispers as to what he was doing." Moving suddenly, she scares me when she leans forward and grabs my hand. "I swear to you, if I had known, I would have put a stop to it. Even if he was my son, I never would have let that continue on. Please, tell me you believe me?"

Her pleading eyes full of unshed tears break my heart. This poor woman is nothing like what I expected and I believe every word she says. "We all have a blind spot when it comes to the people we love. It's natural to think the best of them. I appreciate your candor and I do believe you."

She turns to her lawyer and nods her head. He clears his throat and gets everyone's attention. "Mrs. Montgomery has convinced her husband to drop the case against you. In addition, he has signed a contract that each victim named in the suit against their son will be paid a onetime fee of fifty thousand dollars for emotional damages caused."

Shock runs through my body. There is elation, of course, hearing my case is being dropped but to hear that they are going to help out the girls is more than I could have ever hoped for. Tears freely roll down my face. Casey rubs my back and I know he's trying to comfort me without it looking too personal.

"My husband has admitted he knew about Dirk's actions. I have filed for a divorce and I am leaving town. I always knew a day like this might come when I have to leave quickly so I spent years building up my own account. In lieu of alimony, I made him promise to give the girls their restitution and you have his promise that no one in this town will bother you or your family again. I know this in no way makes up for the harm my family has done but I hope it is a step in the right direction."

"What about you, are you going to be okay?" This poor woman has just told us she is losing her entire family.

"My sister and her family live out in California. I'm going to stay with them while I get settled in. My other children are all fully grown, it's time I take care of myself."

"I wish you all the luck, I truly do."

Her lawyer hands a large stack of papers to Carter. "If you can have each of the families sign these, we'll get everything taken care of quickly. If you'll excuse us, Mrs. Montgomery has a lot to do, as I'm sure you can imagine."

At first I think he is meaning her upcoming move, then I realize he means planning her son's funeral. A wave of nausea hits me along with even more sorrow for this woman.

"Thank you for doing this. I will make sure the families all know what you have done."

She smiles and leaves as gracefully as she had entered. As soon as the door closes, Casey swings me into a hug and kisses me deeply. For a few seconds we forget Carter is in the room until I hear him clear his throat.

"That is a really interesting way to celebrate a win with your client. I hope you don't expect me to do the same." He looks back and forth between us, "I've known from the beginning that you have some serious history but I minded my business as long as it didn't interfere with the case."

"We haven't seen each other in a very long time, thank you for not prying and giving us time to work this out."

"Why don't you two go home and tell your daughter the good news. I will notify the rest of the families that we need them to come here tomorrow."

Carter holds out his hand but I step right past it and give him a hug. "Thank you for sticking by me. I know this was a risk and I appreciate everything you have done for me."

"I said I wanted to go out with a bang, this was definitely worth it. My wife will be happy to hear I'm ready to retire now."

"I wish you both the best of luck, send me a postcard sometime from sunny Florida."

"Will do, and you two better get your stuff worked out and get together. I've never seen two people more perfect for each other, and I have met a lot of couples over the years."

Casey lays his arm across my shoulder and squeezes tight. "Come on, let's tell everyone the good news."

Chapter Thirty-Four

Casey

It's over, it's well and truly over. I had hoped that meeting would be about Brittany's case but it was so much more than I imagined. That woman has done an amazing thing for these girls and most people won't even know.

We share the good news with Maria and the kids as soon as we are in the door. I have never been surrounded by so many crying women in my life. They take turns passing me between them, hugging and crying. Austin, clearly unimpressed with their emotions, salutes me and heads back to the T.V. He has obviously seen this many times and isn't surprised by it.

With my shirt drenched in tears and desperate for a break from being the human tissue, I throw out an idea. "How about we go downstairs and celebrate with a huge feast?"

Cheers all around, at least the tears have started drying up. "If you would like I can pick up your grandmother. I think the family should be together."

"She will love that, I'll call and let her know you are coming." Maria heads to the couch to get her cell phone.

Brittany reaches up on her tiptoes and kisses my cheek, "Thank you for being here, we owe everything to you."

"I will always be here for you and the kids." I pull away and see Kacee standing near us with a huge, goofy grin on her face. I wink before turning back to Brittany. "Can you call downstairs to get us a table for six-thirty and we'll meet you down there?"

Maria hangs up and says Louise will be ready when I get there. She gives Brittany another hug and they all squeal again. "Um, Austin, want to come with me to get Great-Grandma?" A good soldier never leaves a man behind. He jumps up and runs for the door, so I guess that's a yes.

"See you guys in a bit." As I close the door, I hear more screeching. I had no idea they were that worried Brittany was going to jail. How did they manage to cope all this time with that much stress?

"Are they always like that?" I look at Austin, who gives me the most exasperated look a seven-year-old can muster.

"Sometimes Grandma comes over and they all watch shows together. Whenever people kiss, they get like this."

"Sounds like you've had it rough."

"Yeah but it's okay cuz you're here, now I won't be alone."

I'll give this kid credit, from the beginning he's been told I'm going home and even though I know I'm changing my plans, they don't, but he has never given up on me staying here with them.

As we're pulling into Louise's driveway, I realize I am pretty brilliant. Surely with Austin around she won't ask me all kinds of questions about Brittany.

"Lucky me to have two of the city's finest looking gentlemen picking me up for a date."

"You are looking beautiful yourself, Louise." I help her in the passenger seat and climb back in my side. "I hope you are hungry; we are going to eat like royalty tonight."

"It's a good thing I wore the pants with an elastic waist."

This woman is too much, I hope Brittany is just like her someday.

"So what's all the hullabaloo about?"

"Some guy was trying to get Mommy in trouble then he got dead and now everyone's happy."

I nearly swerve off the road. I know we were careful when we talked around him but apparently he picked up on some interesting pieces. I attempt to keep a straight face, "That's the gist of it, I'll let Brittany fill you in on the rest."

"That's a good enough reason for me to eat."

We get to the hotel and sit down minutes before the girls join us. Brittany and Kacee both dressed up, they look absolutely beautiful and it hits me that I am the luckiest man in the world to have these two in my life. Everyone settles in and Louise immediately sets the mood. "Austin says we're eating cuz a guy got dead."

Brittany's horrified face looks at me while everyone else tries to stifle their laughter. I shrug and give my best 'I was as shocked as you were' look.

"That's not exactly true and for the record, we would never celebrate someone else dying."

Louise is filled in on the details as soon as drinks are ordered. I didn't realize there was a tension hanging over everyone up till now. The obvious relaxation in all of them puts them in great moods. While we wait for dinner, Kacee tells me a lot of the girls have been texting her asking if she heard about Dirk's accident and if she knows what the meeting at Carter's is about. We had already agreed she wouldn't tell any of them about the deals yet. It's better if everything is handled through the lawyers.

As soon as I take a bite of my appetizer, Louise makes me choke. "So Casey, I guess this means you will be going home soon?"

Silence deadens the table; everyone stares at me intently, wanting to know what my answer will be. Once I get the food down, I clear my throat. "Well, all of you are out here," I grab Kacee's hand and smile at her, "I am definitely going to make a few changes so I can get to know these two better." I try not to look over at Brittany, I don't want to give away any of my plans.

"That's good to hear, I'd hate to think we won't be seeing you anymore."

"Sorry to disappoint, Louise, but you aren't getting rid of me that easily."

She smiles mischievously before returning to her soup. She sure does know how to rile a crowd, doesn't she?

The rest of the meal goes off flawlessly with plenty of food, wine and laughs. Austin yawns in his dish of chocolate ice cream. "I'll take him upstairs so you guys don't have to rush." Kacee puts her napkin on the table and stands up.

"Thank you, sweetie, we'll be up soon."

The kids hug everyone goodnight before heading up.

"Should we order another round of drinks?" I motion for the waiter.

"Actually, I think it's time for us to get going, too. I'll drop Mom on my way home."

"Thanks, Maria, I appreciate that."

As soon as they are gone, nervousness floods my system. I'm alone with Brittany for the first time since last night.

"I can't believe I am going to wake up tomorrow and there will be no trials hanging over my head. It still hasn't set in that it's really over." She nervously rolls the stem of her wine glass between her fingers. "I guess this means the kids and I can move back to our apartment."

The smile fades from my face, I hadn't thought of that. "If you want to do that you can, but how about you guys stay here for the rest of the week then Friday morning we can fly home for the weekend? I really want my parents to meet the kids."

"You know what, I haven't had a weekend off in sixteen years. Why don't you take the time to bond with the kids and I'll do, well, pretty much anything I want?"

"If you are sure that's what you want then I'll get everything booked tonight. Why don't you stay here at the hotel and take advantage of the spa?"

"That actually sounds like a great idea."

She looks so beautiful in the dim light of the restaurant, glowing from relief and happiness. Without a thought, my hands slide into her hair and pull her face toward mine. "Stay with me tonight?"

Her eyes widen slightly, "I was hoping you might ask me that. How about I sneak in after the kids are asleep?"

"It's a date." I sign the check and hold my hand out for her to stand. Arm in arm, we walk back to the room. I didn't mean for this to happen but god, I'm glad it did.

Chapter Thirty-Five

Brittany

The last few days have been magical; every dream I've ever had of Casey is coming true. We are living like a family and everyone is happy about it. Well, as happy as we can be considering I am sneaking in his room after midnight and getting up at five-thirty in the morning to beat Kacee up.

Last night was exciting; the kids have never been on a plane before so getting them to sleep was tougher than usual. They are all packed and leaving for the airport in a few minutes. I still can't believe I am going a whole weekend without seeing my kids. I am trying not to worry about the reaction their new grandparents are going to give them. Casey is adamant they will accept them readily; I think he's overly optimistic.

"If everyone is ready, we should have enough time to drop your mom at work before heading for the airport."

Austin already has his backpack on and is ready by the door. I kiss each kid goodbye and give them the usual stern reminders like 'Listen to Casey' and 'Mind your manners'. I hug Casey but resist the urge to kiss him in front of the kids. They rush out the door first, Casey takes advantage and pinches my butt as I pass by.

The ride in is animated as Austin is nearly bouncing in his seat. With one final quick kiss for each kid, I wave as they pull away.

"Where are they off to?" I jump at Sharon's voice right behind me.

"Holy shit, you scared the crap out of me."

"Sorry," she doesn't look sorry at all. "Now that the case is over, Casey wanted to take the kids home to South Carolina for the weekend."

"So does that mean we're having a girl's night Saturday? Dinner, drinks, and whatever else we can come up with?"

I had planned to spend the weekend relaxing and reading those letters that have been taunting me in my desk.

"Come on, you never get adult time, I'll buy the first round of drinks." I can't resist the hopeful look on her face.

"Sure, we can do Saturday night." She links her arm through mine and squeezes with excitement as she pulls me into the building.

The day goes quickly as I get texts as Casey and the kids get to the airport, take off, and land. So far no calls from Kacee about evil grandparents so maybe I was overreacting. By the end of the day my nerves have continued to build. The box of letters has been in my desk drawer taunting me almost like they have a heartbeat and want me to remember they are there. I grab the box and head out. Thankfully Sharon is so distracted by making plans for Saturday, she doesn't even question it.

The taxi ride to the hotel doesn't take long, and on my way to the elevator I see one of the front desk clerks waving to me.

"Good evening, Mrs. Sanders. Your husband wanted me to let you know he made an appointment for you at the spa tonight at six p.m."

That sly dog didn't trust me to pamper myself...he was probably right. I glance at my cell phone, that only gives me thirty minutes to change and be back downstairs. I guess the letters will wait a bit longer.

"Thank you for letting me know."

She smiles and returns to her post as I get on the elevator. Having someone else look out for me is kinda nice, I could get used to this.

I toss the box of letters on the coffee table and rush to clean up and throw on a comfortable sundress. I grab the room service menu and place an order to be delivered at eight-fifteen. I'm sure they got a kick out of me ordering only one meal with an entire bottle of wine. This is my weekend and I'm going to enjoy it.

The hostess at the spa greets me warmly and offers a menu of services. I choose the deep tissue massage/facial combo and follow her to my room. She shows me where to lock up my clothes and leaves me to undress. I change quickly and climb under the blankets; I've never been naked in front of a total stranger before. Unless you count the nurses from labor and delivery but come on, I was way too distracted by my innards being ripped apart to care.

A young, soft spoken woman knocks and enters. I hear soft music come on right before she explains what she is going to do. A few minutes later, she puts cool pads over my eyes and I do the one thing I haven't done in years. I shut my brain off and let myself go with the feelings.

Two amazing hours later, my body is relaxed and I feel great. I get back to the hotel room minutes before dinner arrives. The aroma from the steak smells heavenly, my stomach immediately growls with need. I find a movie on T.V. quickly and dig in. Two glasses of wine later and my entire meal consumed, the box of letters catches my eye. Being the coward I am, I pour another glass of wine and dig into the chocolate cake I ordered at the very last second in a moment of weakness. I take my time enjoying every bite. Yes, this is stalling, but it tastes so good.

Finally, the movie ends. I grab the bottle of half gone wine, the box of letters and head to Casey's room. I was smart and had put the do not disturb sign up yesterday. I wanted to sleep in his bed and smell him on the pillows. It's a sadistic kind of torture but one I will gladly endure.

I climb into the center of the king-sized bed, stuff the pillows into a pile and sit against the headboard with the box in between my legs. With another large gulp of liquid courage, I lift the lid off with shaking hands. The envelopes vary in size and color but they are neatly stacked and tied with a red ribbon. Grandma really did take care of these, I'll have to remember to thank her later.

The first envelope is written with the messy handwriting I remember Casey having. I pull out a sheet of lined notebook paper, the edges torn raggedly. His handwriting is a frantic scramble. It's obvious this was written emotionally and not carefully.

Tears instantly well in my eyes, it's dated two weeks after we left.

July 21st, 1990

Britt,

I don't know what to do. You disappeared and no one will help me find you. I went to the police but they said you aren't considered missing since you guys let the landlord know you were leaving. I don't understand what happened, we had plans. I need to know you are okay. Please call me and let me know where you are. I can come get you, just talk to me please. I don't know what I did but I promise to make it up to you.

Where are you?
Casey

The desperation and despair rips my heart to shreds. I can't believe he went to the police; I had hoped my note to him would have been enough to keep him from getting too upset. With another gulp of wine, I grab the next envelope. This one is dated six weeks after we left.

August 17th, 1990
Britt,

Why haven't you called me? This address is the only thing I have to go on. I am hoping it took you guys a while to drive there and you will call me after you get this. I need to know you are okay, please let me know what happened.

I need you,
Casey

Desperate to get through the pain, I grab the next envelope dated three months after we left.

October 10th, 1990
Brittany,

I assume by now you would have gotten to this address if it's where you were going. I haven't heard from you so I assume you aren't there. This is the only information I have from your family; I can't give up hope that my letters will find you. I've begged my parents to find you, we have the money, but they say it's for the best and refuse to help. They are keeping a close eye on me, I think they are afraid I'm going to hurt myself. I won't do that, I have to find you and I can't do that if I'm gone. Please let me know you are okay.

I love you,
Casey

Holy shit, I broke that beautiful boy. I know I had it rough in those first few months but I had my mom and grandma to help me get through. He had no one, his parents were never nurturing people. I did this to him, I tortured the boy I loved.

The next four letters are all written over the next eight months. His handwriting has smoothed back to his original handwriting. The paper is now nicer paper. He goes on to document his senior year for me. I'm devastated to read he had skipped prom and barely participated in other events. Thankfully he kept his grades up well enough and he tells me he is still going to Harvard. I can tell his inner voice has changed, his letter's lack emotion. I almost prefer the panic to the broken.

His last letter of high school has a small graduation picture inside. My eyes blur again with tears staring at his beautiful face. We missed so much, can we really get past all of that?

I grab the bottle of wine for another drink before continuing on only to find it completely empty. I guess I have to do the rest of this on my own.

From this point on the letters become more sporadic; they come roughly twice a year while he's in college. His handwriting has matured and I actually manage to laugh reading about some of the antics his friends pulled. Each letter had a few pictures in it from important events that had happened since the previous letter. I'm a little overwhelmed by the idea of Casey sitting at his desk listing out his life like he's catching up an old friend who is going to write back. For the most part the letters are positive, but he does mention therapy and a group he attends where people talk about people they've lost.

I knew all along where he was and that he was okay; he treated me like I had died. He has every right to hate me, I don't understand why he doesn't.

After college the letters switch to yearly. His handwriting has become slanted and beautiful. They are filled with stories about town, people we went to school with but small tidbits jump out at me more than the rest.

July 8th, 1997

I met a girl, she seems nice. Of course my parents love her. They are pushing me to go out with her. Why can't they understand she isn't you?

Forever Yours,
Casey

July 8th, 1998

My therapist says it's time for me to stop looking for you. It's not healthy and I need to move on. I know he's right but I'm not sure I can do it. I know you are out there.

Forever Yours,
Casey

July 8th, 1999

Monica and I have been dating for a while now, everyone is pushing me to propose. She's great and she will make a great wife so why am I not more excited? I do admit I love her, maybe this can work out after all. I pray you are doing well wherever you are.

Forever Yours,
Casey

July 8th, 2000

I asked Monica to move in with me, she said yes. My job at the firm is going great, I have a really good shot of going far. You would be so proud of me; I've accomplished everything we dreamed of. Maybe I am ready to make all this work. You will always hold a special place in my heart but I think I need to give Monica all of me and not just the shell I've been hiding in.

Forever Yours,
Casey

I asked Monica to marry me, my parents are thrilled. I am too, she is so good to me. I hope you are doing well and have everything you desire.

Forever Yours,
Casey

July 8th, 2002

The firm has made me a partner, I'm the youngest in company history! I know you are proud of me; I hope you are reaching your dreams, too.

Forever Yours,
Casey

July 8th, 2004

My parents are pushing me for a wedding. They want it done before I run for District Attorney. You heard that right, I've been asked to run. I can't believe it either. This is so much more than we ever imagined, I wish you were here to celebrate it with me. I drove by your old apartment building the other day. You would be shocked at how run down it has become. I am glad you got out of there, I'm sure you are happy wherever you are.

Forever Yours,
Casey

When the last letter is done, I let my head fall back against the headboard. That was even more painful than I expected it to be. My eyes feel swollen and my throat has a huge lump in it but I made it through them all. It was like ripping a band aid off, just get it done quickly.

Stifling a huge yawn, I look at the alarm clock and realize it's almost four in the morning. Maybe I didn't get through them as quickly as I thought I did. As carefully as possible, I gather the letters and put them on the side table. I need to get sleep; I just pray I drank enough to not have dreams from everything I've read.

Chapter Thirty-Six

Casey

The kids were great on the plane, Kacee's face was hysterical when she saw the flaps move back on the wings as we landed. She thought the plane was coming apart, I thought she was going to break my hand squeezing it so hard.

I enjoyed driving them around the city, showing them where their mom grew up, where we went to school and our favorite hang outs. I think it was good for Kacee to see where she came from.

As expected, their jaws drop as we pull down the drive toward my parents' house. The house is huge; most people would call it a mansion. For me it was never home, just a place I slept at and waited to turn eighteen and get out on my own. Don't get me wrong, my parents aren't bad people, they just never felt particularly fond of parenting.

I pull under the alcove and get out. Looking back, I see the kids haven't moved, they are just staring at the house.

"It's okay, they are going to love you guys."

Kacee gets out first and holds Austin's hand as we head inside. I motion for them to follow me as we head toward the study.

"Hello, anyone here? I'm home."

"In here, dear."

I turn the corner to the study and my mother's large smile disappears as she stares at the kids. She turns to my dad and sighs.

"So you found them." My father words crash around me.

They are both staring at the kids.

"Care to explain what you mean?"

"Melissa." My mother calls out for the maid. "Melissa, can you take the children to the kitchen and give them something to eat?"

Both kids look to me before moving. "It's okay, go ahead. Her chocolate cake is amazing; she usually keeps it on hand."

Austin looks excitedly to Melissa, who winks and smiles at him. Kacee isn't so easy to distract, she looks back at my parents before giving me a questioning look.

"It's okay, I'll be along soon. Make sure Austin doesn't eat all the cake before I get there."

She nods reluctantly before following Melissa out. Steeling my shoulders for battle, I sit on the couch across from my parents and stare them down without saying a word. I am not going to break first.

"How's Brittany doing?"

"I think the better question is why don't you look surprised to see those kids? I assume you know who they are, now tell me how long you have known about them."

"We've always known about them. You were such a mess after Brittany left, we hired a private investigator to find out what happened. He brought us pictures showing she was very pregnant." Mom cowers slightly under my intense stare; she looks to Dad to finish.

"Your mother and I made a tough decision. We didn't want you derailing your future so we pretended ignorance. I had no doubt you would get over everything after a while. I do admit it took a lot longer than we expected, but it worked. You have everything you wanted and a beautiful fiancée ready to give you a family of your own."

"That's the root of the issue, isn't it? I have everything *you* wanted but I already have a family. If you will excuse me, I'm taking my children and leaving."

"Honey, please, stay and talk to us."

The feelings of betrayal are overwhelming. Without looking back, I head to the kitchen and find the kids finishing up their cake.

"Thanks for the cake, Melissa. Come on, guys, it's time to go."

"Is everything okay, Dad?"

Melissa's eyes bulge, at least she didn't know about my parents' deception either. "Everything's fine, we'll come back another time."

I stomp out the door, the kids following close behind. I don't even look at my parents as they stare at us from the hallway.

For a minute we sit in the car. I had planned to leave the kids here while I talked to Monica but now I need a new plan. I drive to the Hilton by my office and grab a two-bedroom suite like before.

"Let's put our bags away then go get some dinner. I need to run an errand later so you guys can rent a movie in the room while I'm gone."

Both kids have been pretty silent since we left my parents. I feel terrible they had to go through that. I'm sure I'll get a call from a very unhappy Brittany once she finds out about it. I text her we're getting dinner and then turning in for the night.

As dinner goes on, the kids relax and are back in good moods. Now that everything has changed with my parents, all my plans for the weekend are out the window. I give the kids a few options and we make plans for tomorrow. I'm going to have to talk to my parents again but first I want them to think on it for a while.

Before going back to our room, we grab drinks and snacks to fill up the fridge. Anxious to get my next errand over with, I get them settled in with the movie and head to my apartment with Monica.

She's working on her computer when I get there. My heart clenches when she hugs and kisses me. She deserves so much more than I have given her and definitely more than I can give her now that my life has completely changed.

"I'm so glad you are finally home; I didn't think that case was ever going to end. Grab a beer and come tell me about it." She grabs her wine glass and heads to the couch. Resigning myself to the conversation, I grab a beer and sit across from her.

"What's wrong? You seem down."

"When we met, I was leaving a survivors meeting. I told you about my girlfriend who I had lost."

She leans back against the couch and folds her arms across her chest. Her body language says she already knows where this is going.

"I got a call from her mother that they were in Utah and they needed my help. I couldn't believe she was alive; I took off to finally get the answers I've needed for the last sixteen years. Little did I expect she would tell me we have a daughter together."

I look up at her face and see her eyes widen, she clearly wasn't expecting me to say that. "Brittany, my missing girlfriend, had been wrongfully arrested and was in real trouble of going to jail. A lot happened while I was out there but we managed to get the case dismissed. You wouldn't believe the crazy family who is running that city, they are worse than anyone we have around here."

"Did you get to meet your daughter?"

"Yes and she is amazing. I brought her and her little brother here. I wanted them to meet my parents."

"Is Brittany here as well?" I can see the worry in her eyes, if only she knew this was going to get worse.

"No, she stayed home."

"You're going back to her, aren't you?"

It's my turn to look surprised, she asked the question so matter-of-factly. "I have never given myself to you completely. I couldn't, part of me had died all those years ago and I never fully healed. Being back with Brittany woke that side of me again."

A single tear rolls down her cheek. Kneeling in front of her, I grab her hands. "I swear when I went out there it was to get answers and help her out. I know this isn't fair to you but I have to get to know her and our daughter."

"What about the firm?"

"I'm hoping they will agree to let me open an office for them out there. If not, I'll open my own practice. I am so sorry to do this to you. I want you to keep the ring and do whatever you want with it. I'll also pay off the rent for the rest of the lease. Please, tell me you don't hate me?"

With a final swipe of tears from her cheeks, she leans forward and kisses me deeply on the lips. "I always knew I only had half of your heart. I was okay with that; you are worth it. I don't want to lose you but I know I don't have a choice. You have to go where you are complete. I'll go stay at Stephanie's this weekend so you can move your things out."

Her fingers glide through my hair for a brief few seconds before she stands and walks to our room. Without a backward glance, she closes herself in, and that's my cue to leave. Love is a fickle beast; it demands pain in equal measure to elation.

Chapter Thirty-Seven

Brittany

My eyes won't open, they are caked in sleep and dried up tears. At first I think the pounding is in my head, but eventually I figure out someone is knocking on the door. My head throbs as I sit up, I grab the robe hanging behind the door and call out that I'm coming. Through the peephole I see a woman around my mother's age wearing a navy suit. Running my fingers through my hair, I open the door.

"Ms. Celdonio?"

"Yes?"

"My name is Leslie Sampson, Mr. Sanders' assistant. By your look of confusion, I am guessing he didn't tell you I was coming?"

"I'm sorry, he didn't. Come inside, please." She follows me to the couches. Embarrassed, I grab my dinner tray from last night and move it to the kitchenette area. "Sorry about the mess, I fell asleep right after dinner last night."

"No need to explain."

"If you don't mind me asking, Casey is back in South Carolina so why are you out here?"

"He called me a few days ago and let me know that he wants to buy a house out here. He gave me his base requirements and I've gathered several properties that may work. Mr. Sanders said you know the area well and you would be able to pick the perfect house."

"He wants me to pick out his house for him?"

"Yes, ma'am. Once you have a decision I will set up the contract with the realtor and he will take care of it."

"That's awful trusting of him."

She smiles mischievously and shrugs. "If you are free today, I can wait in my room down the hall while you get ready? You can come get me in room 1409 when you are done."

"Sure, give me twenty minutes." As soon as she's out the door, I grab my cell phone and call Casey.

He picks up on the second ring. "Oh crap, I meant to call you last night."

"I had a visit with your assistant, she had an interesting request."

"I'm sorry, things got a little crazy around here last night and I completely forgot to call."

"Are the kids okay?"

"Oh yeah, sorry, the kids are great. We drove around your old neighborhood, had dinner, they rented a movie. It was great, I am really glad you agreed to let them come with me."

"I'm glad it's going well. Now explain why I am picking out your house for you?"

"I don't know the area and you do. I trust your judgment and you know me well."

That's a lot of faith considering I haven't seen him in years. The letters helped me catch up on a lot of his life but that doesn't mean he hasn't changed. At least I'll have Mrs. Sampson to help me.

"I'll give it my best shot but I really think you should see the house before you buy it, okay?"

"If that will make you more comfortable then I will gladly go see it first."

With a resigned groan, I mumble, "Fine, she's waiting for me so I need to get ready. Tell the kids I love them and I want Kacee to call me later."

"Will do but before you go, did you sleep naked in my bed last night?"

"Goodbye, Casey." I wait till after I've hung up to chuckle, I don't want him to know how adorable I think he is.

As the shower heats up, I catch a glimpse of my reflection in the mirror. That is one terrible first impression I made. Hopefully the shower will do wonders for what the wine and letters did to me last night.

Twenty-five minutes later, I'm dressed and feel much more presentable. I grab Mrs. Sampson on my way down to the bakery in the lobby. We grab coffee and bagels then head to a table to review the folder in her arm.

"I tried to map out the houses as best I could. If there are any you think we should take off the table immediately, let me know and I'll toss them. If you can help me put them in order, I'll call the realtor and tell her which house to meet us at first."

It only took flipping through three listings to see that he is not buying a simple home. They are all four to five bedroom houses in very affluent neighborhoods. I figure he would want Kacee and possibly Austin to stay with him sometimes but this seems excessive. And I'm not about to assume he's thinking of me staying there. We only reconnected a couple of weeks ago and he has a lot going on back home.

Once I have a final list of houses in order, Mrs. Sampson calls the realtor and we head out. It only takes three hours to get through five houses. All of them are gorgeous and will be great for Casey. The realtor treats us to lunch before finishing up the tour with three more houses.

Exhausted and ready to sit for a while, we tell the realtor we're going to discuss and call her soon. Back at the hotel bar, we sit down to go through each house.

"These houses are all amazing, how are we supposed to pick?"

"Mr. Sanders will be happy with anything you pick. Why don't you start by listing what you do and don't like about each house?

I understand there will be two children staying there, take into account what they would like.”

Her list idea works perfectly, in under an hour I narrow it down to two houses.

“I can’t choose between these two, I say we let Casey see both of them and he can pick.”

“I think he will be okay with that. I’ll have the realtor set up walkthroughs for tomorrow evening when he is back in town.”

“He told me you keep him in line, I can see why he values you so much.”

“He’s a great boss. You meet a lot of sharks in our business, I’m happy to be working for one of the good guys.”

“So when do you head back to South Carolina?”

“I’ll head back in a few days; I’ll go where Mr. Sanders needs me.”

“If you’d like, I’m having dinner with a friend tonight. We can make it a group outing?”

“Don’t alter your plans for me, I’m happy to hang here.”

“Nonsense. Be ready in an hour, I’ll swing by and get you.”

“That would be lovely, thank you.”

I’m really glad Casey has had this woman in his life. I definitely think she has been good for him and lord knows he deserves some good.

Chapter Thirty-Eight

Casey

"Remember I told you guys I was going to start staying in Utah with you?" I wait for both kids to nod, "I need to go to my apartment and pack up some boxes for the moving company. Is it okay if we get that done before we go out for the day?"

"Sure, we want to help, too, if it means you get to come out sooner." I smile at Kacee's blush; I am glad she seems to be adjusting well to having me in her life.

The movers are waiting for us when we get there. Everyone grabs a box and I point out what they should pack. I decide to leave everything for Monica that isn't personal, so it doesn't take long. Sad to say my entire life fits into ten boxes.

As the movers carry the last boxes out, I see my parents coming in. Kacee gives me a look, I know she gets the gist of what is going on. I smile to reassure her everything is fine.

"Kacee, can you and Austin watch T.V. for a few minutes?" I motion my parents to follow me out on the balcony. Again, I sit and stare at them, refusing to be the first to speak.

"What are the boxes for?"

"I'm moving to Utah to be with Brittany and the kids."

I'm surprised to see tears spring into my mother's eyes. Dad shakes his head angrily.

"Damn it, Casey, you can't take off and leave everything behind. You've worked too hard to let all of this go."

"None of it means anything if I'm not with Brittany. You let me suffer for sixteen years and you knew all this time where they were. How am I supposed to forgive you?"

My mom grabs my hand desperately, "You have to believe us. We made sure she was okay. Once we knew where she was, we hired a detective out there to send us updates and pictures. If we ever thought they needed anything, we would have helped them. They turned out great, we have been very proud watching Kacee grow up."

"That's great, I'm glad you got to enjoy watching my daughter grow up. You never gave me love and attention as a kid and you've robbed me of it as an adult."

I know the words are hurtful but I won't take them back, not even when my mother looks like I might as well have slapped her.

"The kids and I are flying home tomorrow morning. You can get rid of the P.I. I will send pictures."

"Casey, please don't do this, don't leave like this. We've made mistakes, we know that. After a few years, we realized we had dug ourselves into a hole and we didn't know how to get out. We don't want to lose you and we want those children in our life."

My father has been silent through this, I don't know what he is thinking. "What about Brittany? You never gave her a chance. You wrote her off from day one." I stare at my dad, demanding he be the one to answer.

"We were wrong about her, I'm man enough to admit that. She has done a great job getting her life together and raising our grandchild. Add her to the list of regrets we have. We would be proud to have her as a daughter-in-law."

I know that took a lot for my father to admit, I nod in acceptance.

"Will you introduce us? We'd like to finally meet them."

"I will but I'm warning you now, they have never known anything but love so you will not hurt them. If you are going to be in their lives, you need to start acting like real grandparents." I wait till both nod before taking them inside to meet their grandchildren.

Chapter Thirty-Nine

Brittany

Two days in a row waking up confused and hung over is not a good thing. I get one weekend to myself and I become a raging party girl. Sitting up, I realize I had slept on the couch and after a quick sweep of the area, I see Leslie passed out on the other couch and Sharon curled up on some cushions on the ground. She's sure going to be sore when she wakes up. With a groan I lay back and try to remember how we got here.

After dinner last night, we took our little party to a club. We danced, we laughed, we drank copious amounts of alcohol. Once Leslie got drunk, she admitted Casey told her he was breaking up with Monica this weekend. This was the final cloud that had been hanging over me, instant relief flooded me at the idea of him being available again.

Alcohol is never good during an emotionally charged time in your life. I remember with a groan that I invited both ladies back to the hotel and I spilled my guts to them. I told them about leaving him while pregnant, the letters he wrote me, the need burning deep within me to be with him.

I sit up again and look over to the coffee table. Lying there are a couple of Casey's white undershirts. We apparently used lipstick and wrote a sign. I had to turn my head a few times till I could make out what it says, "Will you go to prom with me?"

The memory floods my mind. I pulled out the letter where Casey says he skipped prom. They thought it was as sad as I did and we all cried for him. In the sober light of day, I realize what idiots we must have looked like. Sharon reminded me that Kacee's school prom was coming up and I should ask Casey to be my date, as a chaperone, but still we would finally be getting our prom. Apparently we liked the idea, we have the shirts to prove it.

I hear a lot of moaning from the other couch as Leslie sits up and holds her head. I use my foot and nudge Sharon till she joins us in our suffering.

"Oh my god, did we die last night?" Sharon shoves the pillow over her eyes and moans.

"We definitely didn't die or we wouldn't feel this miserable." Leslie looks up at me from blood shot eyes. "I'm a grandmother, you know. I haven't done something like this in thirty years."

"I don't think any of us have ever partied that hard."

Leslie catches sight of our artwork and bursts into laughter. Sharon sits up to find out what's so funny when she sees them, too. "I hope those aren't like Armani shirts, I can't afford to replace them if so."

Leslie laughs until she cries and soon we all sound like crazy people. Gasping for air, I finally settle down.

"Thank you, ladies, for putting up with me last night. I realize now I way over shared my problems."

"Are you kidding me? It was better than any soap opera or book I've ever read."

"I'm glad my life could entertain you." I toss my pillow at Sharon and stick my tongue out.

"Well, the way I see it; we have less than two hours to put our plan into motion."

"What plan?" I stare quizzically at Leslie who looks at me like I've lost my mind.

"The plan for you to ask Casey to the prom, of course."

"We weren't serious about that, were we?"

"We need better signs but I'm with Leslie, we need to get cleaned up and get you to the airport."

Both women share determined looks before springing into action. Sharon forces me to the bathroom and tells me to get in the shower. By the time I come out, the living room is spotless and Sharon tells me Leslie is showering in her room and will be back soon.

I give Sharon some clothes and wait nervously while she gets ready. In no time at all they are ready to go and I feel like throwing up.

"I don't know, guys. He has been single for what, twenty-four hours? How do we know he wants this?"

I get looks from them that clearly say I'm an idiot. "Casey has been all about the job for the last six years. He is quitting to move out here and be near you. Heck, he hired me away and I'm moving out here to work for him. If you don't think that is a man in love then you are dumber than I thought."

Sharon and I both stare at Leslie. "I didn't know he was coming here full-time, he never said. Don't you have family back home?"

"Nope, my daughter and grandkids are in Arizona. The way I look at it, I'll be even closer to them now. Plus, I think of Casey as a son, I wouldn't want to leave him."

"That's good enough for me. Now grab your purse, we have posters to buy."

Chapter Forty

Casey

I won't say I've forgiven my parents; they have a lot to atone for. However, I have nothing to complain about as far as their treatment of the kids yesterday. With time I think they can learn to be good grandparents.

As soon as the plane touches down, I turn on my cell and text Brittany that we've landed. After being with her for three weeks straight, I find my skin crawling at being away from her so long. It's as if my body knows we found her and it doesn't want to lose sight of her again.

Mrs. Sampson told me the house search has been narrowed down to two. I can't wait to tell the kids and take them to pick out their home. I pray Brittany feels the same as I do and will move in with me.

"Are you guys excited to see your mom?"

Austin's wide smile is all the answer I need, he missed her as much as I did. On the shuttle from the gate to the main terminal, I check my phone twice more. Brittany hasn't responded. I hope she didn't sleep in and forget she's picking us up.

There is a large crowd of people waiting for relatives when we get there. I can't find her in the crowd. Kacee spots her first and covers her mouth as she gasps.

"Do you see her?"

She points to a group off to the right holding large posters in the air. As we get closer, my mouth goes dry. Standing there looking beautiful is Mrs. Sampson, Sharon, Brittany's mother, grandmother and of course, Brittany. The signs read, "Will you...go to...prom...with me?"

Brittany is biting her lip; I can see the nervousness on her face. She never did like attention and right now she has a lot of people gathered around us watching.

"Casey Sanders, I wasn't there to take you to your senior prom. I want to make that up to you. Will you go to prom with me?"

She read the letters. I remember writing about skipping the prom. At a loss for words, unusual for a person in my line of work, I lift her into a hug and plant a kiss on her gorgeous mouth.

"Is that a yes? Will you be my prom date?"

"I'll be forever yours."

ABOUT THE AUTHOR

Cassidy lives in the Tampa, Florida area with her high school sweetheart, their three children and one crazy dog. She loves reading and going to the movies but not nearly as much as she enjoys watching her kids either playing ball or performing with one of their instruments. She also loves to travel and hopes to one day watch a baseball game in every MLB stadium in the country.

To learn more about Cassidy please visit her online at www.cassidykoconnor.com.

You can also find her on Facebook at www.facebook.com/cassidykoconnorauthor

She always welcomes new friends and encourages readers to reach out to her.